The Church:
A Workshop of Salvation

The Church:
A Workshop of Salvation

Alastair Redfern

2016

The Church: A Workshop of Salvation— published by the Rev. Dr. Ashish Amos of the Indian Society for Promoting Christian Knowledge (ISPCK), Post Box 1585, Kashmere Gate, Delhi-110006.

© Author, 2016

ISBN: 978-81-8465-555-1

ISPCK, Post Box 1585, 1654, Madarsa Road, Kashmere Gate, Delhi-110006 • *Tel:* 23866323

e-mail: ashish@ispck.org.in • ella@ispck.org.in
website: www.ispck.org.in

Contents

Preface

By almost every measure, the Christian church in Western Societies seems to be on the backfoot – in retreat and often in decline. This retreat involves numbers of adherents, intellectual credibility, societal contribution and organisational coherence. If a credible public witness and a persuasive personal journey is to be offered in such testing times, there is an urgent need to read the context of debilitating pressures, and to restore confidence in the resources with which the church has been gifted.

In terms of the context, an interesting indicator in the twenty first century is the concern to combat the evils of Modern Slavery. There is an increasing solidarity around the view that slavery is an abusive situation to be eradicated. Our concern is to provide for every human being, its opposite – freedom. This is the increasingly powerful trajectory of western civilisation, and the grid of modernity by which almost everything is measured. Thus, since the French revolution in 1789 and what is now called the Age of Enlightenment, civilisation for human beings has been linked closely with the centrality of 'freedom'. This agenda has been steadily pursued in relation to personal freedom, focussed in the twenty first century upon Human Rights and the substantiating role of the United Nations.

There has been a key and largely successful shift towards political freedom. However, despite the moves towards universal suffrage in many nations, political power remains fully in the control of wealthy elites, and in the United Kingdom this reality of exclusion for most people from the practicalities of politics has resulted in widespread cynicism amongst the so called electorate and a compensatory over-emphasis upon personal space and liberty.

Least progress has been made in the area of economic freedom, since the increasing inequalities within societies, and the bread and circuses approach of the market through the tool of 'fashion' combine to exclude huge number of citizens from a fair share of the products of a national economy.

The most complex area of freedom for modern society is that of the spiritual. In one sense the privatisation of religion seems to have created a safe space for individual liberty in spiritual matters – but this process, by definition, excludes the spiritual from public life, except in the ritual of certain public occasions, and thus denies any freedom for spiritual principles to be made manifest more broadly.

The root of all freedom is the person – the soul that hopes, fears, regrets, seeks – within a universalising sense of being part of something much greater, something to do with the power and purpose of our life. The agenda of the heart is a spiritual force and seeks a spiritual freedom to be, to become, to connect, to pursue completion. The language and register is always richer than the capacity of the mind to describe or capture these intuitions. The western heritage still echoes with an ecclesiastical solution to this dilemma – the structures and sacraments of a church that can give focus, while owning the need for more particular implementation of this spiritual force through political, economic and other processes. There has been a dynamic between the encouragement and critique of the bigger picture (the arena of the spiritual life) and the working out of practical ways of earthing these elements into the limited contexts of human understanding and capacities. In the age of the modern and the postmodern, this dynamic could be perceived to have been settled by the exclusion of religion from the public square and the increasingly unchallenged supremacy of human science and reason.

This process began with the Enlightenment, which served to focus upon the human minds ability to rationalise and order life according to the most pragmatic criteria. Description became the method of discerning what seemed to be observable and therefore 'true' for that moment. Analysis provided tools for identifying possibilities and priorities for the future.

The underlying spiritual principle became a common bond in generalised faith that evolution provided progress, despite occasional setbacks. The emphasis upon the discernible served to put the individual in the centre of each picture, as the arbiter of 'truth' from their particular perspective. The spiritual element of human being was a mysterious inner core that could work outwards to witness into the world, according to its own particular views and values. The spiritual thus became a market place crowded with attempts to negotiate and build working alliances between such autonomous agents to achieve effective outcomes in the everyday world. In this sense the spiritual is simply one factor amongst many within the current obsession with politics and economics.

The result of these developments has been the marginalisation of 'church' as a public institution, and a tendency for churches to focus upon consumer demand – the fulfilment of increasingly demanding individuals.

However, according to the Christian gospel, the spiritual is the light that lightens every creature, the inner presence and power of the Creator God in His creatures, especially in His children. This indwelling makes every individual dependent, totally – on this gift and its working out in the totality of human lives. This is the key to Christian life, and especially its public expression in the church. Not just for the working of the Gospel in personal lives, but as a model or workshop for public life to be refined, renewed and redeemed.

The theme of 'slavery' is especially poignant. In contemporary worldly terms it is a sign of the most horrific abuse of vulnerable people – for the sake of profit and power. In terms of the Christian tradition, slavery denotes a potent paradox – the power of the One who chooses the lowest place of unconditional service to become the Saviour and overseer of the proper fulfilment of human life. Slavery as a tool of salvation rather than as a crime against humanity.

The following chapters seek to explore the outlines for such an ecclesial workshop – a working church offering signs of the story of salvation, through a spirituality of seeking to offer the slavery of self-sacrificing service. (John 13:12-27).

Introduction

This book forms part of what has emerged as a trilogy. Three endeavours to explore the spirituality and missionary witness of sacrifice and service: the way of Jesus Christ in a complex and contradictory world.

Early in 2015, in order to encourage prayerful preparation and reflection for a General Election in the United Kingdom scheduled for later that year, I produced a short text 'The Word on the Street' (ISPCK 2015) – inviting Christians and others to work together to identify concerns and priorities at local levels that could become the stuff of effective engagement with the issues facing not just our own society, but also those embedded in the cultural values and political practices that seemed to have become normative for providing a means of dealing with them.

The book, and an accompanying workbook, took the theme of 'The English Parish and the Future of Politics'. It offered tools for local people to connect with the concerns of their communities and together try to craft an Agenda for Action by considering seven common contemporary challenges. The aim was to encourage the practicing of local politics. The focus was upon sacrifice and service through the exercise of Christian citizenship.

A second book, 'Peace that Passes Understanding – spiritual wholeness in a divided world' (ISPCK 2015) attempted to look at the personal path of a spirituality which might emerge into the transformative Christian citizenship explored in 'The Word on the Street'. The aim was to explore in particular the Pauline dynamic of being called to live 'in Christ'.

The present work looks at the implications for our understanding of 'church', especially the corporate witness of Christians manifested through membership of the Body of Christ. The aim is to outline for our contemporary context an ecclesiology that could enable both an outward witness of Christian citizenship, and an inner journey of nurture for the soul called to live in Christ, through the embrace of His Body the Church.

CHAPTER – 1

The Call to Change

"Brothers and fathers, listen to the defence that I now make before you."

² When they heard him addressing them in Hebrew, they became even more quiet. Then he said:

³ "I am a Jew, born in Tarsus in Cilicia, but brought up in this city at the feet of Gamaliel, educated strictly according to our ancestral law, being zealous for God, just as all of you are today. ⁴ I persecuted this Way up to the point of death by binding both men and women and putting them in prison, ⁵ as the high priest and the whole council of elders can testify about me. From them I also received letters to the brothers in Damascus, and I went there in order to bind those who were there and to bring them back to Jerusalem for punishment.

⁶ "While I was on my way and approaching Damascus, about noon a great light from heaven suddenly shone about me. ⁷ I fell to the ground and heard a voice saying to me, 'Saul, Saul, why are you persecuting me?' ⁸ I answered, 'Who are you, Lord?' Then he said to me, 'I am Jesus of Nazareth whom you are persecuting.' ⁹ Now those who were with me saw the light but did not hear the voice of the one who was speaking to me. ¹⁰ I asked, 'What am I to do, Lord?' The Lord said to me, 'Get up and go to Damascus; there you will be told everything that has been assigned to you to do.' ¹¹ Since I could not see because of the brightness of that light, those who were with me took my hand and led me to Damascus.

¹² "A certain Ananias, who was a devout man according to the law and well spoken of by all the Jews living there, ¹³ came to me; and standing beside me, he said, 'Brother Saul, regain your sight!' In that very hour I regained my sight and saw him. ¹⁴ *Then he said, 'The God of our ancestors has chosen you to know his will, to see the Righteous One and to hear his own voice;* ¹⁵ *for you will be his witness to all the world of what you have seen and heard.* ¹⁶ *And now why do you delay? Get up, be baptized, and have your sins washed away, calling on his name.'*

Acts 22:1-16 (NRSV)

Paul has been arrested in the Temple in Jerusalem, accused of "teaching everyone everywhere against our people, our law, and this place; more than that he has actually brought Greeks into the Temple and has defiled this holy place." (Acts 21:28). He begins his response with the word 'listen' – he invites dialogue and an exchange of experiences. He continues by recounting the signs of the light and the voice which changed his life and sense of direction.

The story recognises a traditional starting point – his zeal for "our ancestral law". The key markers in life are those already given – established through the wisdom of the past. Strict education encultured successive generations into a clearly marked out 'territory' which provided the frame for belief and behaviour.

As Paul was journeying to defend the boundaries of this precious territory, and to enforce loyalty and compliance, the light and the voice provided a moment of encounter, a sign, a call towards deterritorialisation. Paul had to confess that though his eyes were open, he could not 'see'. (Acts 9:8). There was something to perceive beyond the territory within which he was so familiar and so secure. Something beyond its detailed laws and controlling perspectives. Beyond the proper attempt to institutionalise what his people had received and achieved thus far, was new territory and possibility. Interestingly this encounter or 'call' takes place on a journey between two settlements: between Jerusalem and Damascus – on an open road.

Yet this was not a purely private personal experience. The light and the voice were from 'the Lord': 'Jesus of Nazareth'. This 'sign' was to be interpreted by Ananias, a devout Christian who was also highly regarded by the Jews. He acknowledged Paul (Saul) as a 'brother' – who is now part of a much bigger enterprise, a witness to the world on behalf of an eternal kingdom – the ultimate in earthly deterritorialisation.

This vocation has not be accessed through a maturing of political achievements in making effective human settlements such as Jerusalem or Damascus. Neither has it been accessed through sophisticated religious practices. The call or vocation emerges on an open road, as sheer gift – though speaking directly to the worries and concerns of the person. Paul (Saul) was very focussed upon the purity of territory and the importance of its maintenance. This manifested itself in a passion for enforcing conformity to what those in authority (at the feet of Gamaliel) knew best. This proper agenda for human flourishing and spiritual faithfulness had become narrowed and prescriptive. On the open road these desires could be touched in a different way.

Those whom Paul was persecuting were known as 'the Way' – a term about direction, and movement. Faith flourishes through a certain fluidity in acknowledging trust in what is yet unseen and thus not fully known. Institutions and ideologies (or theologies) provide temporary moments of focus and clarification, but this very process of solidification to enable something to be better seen and grasped, has the inevitable effect of stopping the flow into an unknown future. The most important part of the typography was not the settlements of Jerusalem or Damascus – but the open road between them.

'Jesus of Nazareth' was thus being persecuted. Jesus – a sign of salvation, health, well-being – temporarily located in the territory of Nazareth, but, as Paul was to discover, more completely known as Jesus the Christ – the One for all others in all places across all time. Jesus – 'the Righteous One' – or as Paul soon learned to say 'He is the Son of God.' (Acts 9:20).

Vocation – call – emerges from a willingness to step out of settled situations, and travel an open road. The call comes as a moment of engagement, through signs – which will need interpreting. It is important to note that Paul struggled to understand the significance of the moment. His eyes were open but he could see nothing (Acts 9:8). He needed an engagement with a stranger wishing to become a friend – a baptised member of the Way. Subsequently Paul re-tells the story of this sign-giving a number of times, as it becomes a continuing tool for re-exploring the direction of his own spiritual journey, and the implications for his contribution to the mission of the wider church.

Such repetition overcomes the predictive logic of a simple analysis that then becomes an answer. By contrast, faith will always seek further elucidation, not just through intellectual expression or religious ritual, but through a commitment of openness to deterritorialisation.

There is a strong spiritual instinct to make religion literal – that is religare – to bind into cohesion. And then, like Paul (Saul), to see mission as the challenge to convert others to accept such 'binding in'. By contrast, the spirituality that emerges from the light and the voice – the vocare of Jesus the Christ – ever seeks to risk stepping outside of 'safe spaces' into the darkness and unknown regions where new things are possible.

The great biblical example is the journey of Abraham with Isaac to the land of Moriah. Abraham took the fire and the knife – the tools of religion. He had a strong sense of ethical values. But when the moment came to receive a sign (enlightenment and the voice) as Kierkegaard shows - he was willing to go beyond the institutionalisation of good values in terms of proper ethical behaviour. He was willing to break the religious commandment by murdering the precious future God had provided him in Isaac. And such willingness to step beyond any sense of settlement and safe territory, into an open road …enabled the sign, the call – to be given. This spiritual process is repeated on Calvary, where the institutionalisation of ethics, politics and religion brings death to the One who was The Way – only for there to be a pause for reflection – the emptiness of Holy Saturday – and then the light and voice – the call to those outside of the tomb, or on their way to Emmaus.

Such a spiritual process provided the framework for vocation. When confronted by challenge the first response is resistance – as in Paul, as in the High Priest and the Pharisees, the response of persecution and defending the hard won territory of settlement.

The tools will be destruction. Such violence needs the response of reflection. Paul blind and subdued for three days. Jesus dying for three hours: entombed for three days. From this sequence of violent defensiveness, and enforced subjugation – can emerge vocation: the light and the voice of a new life and sense of direction. The tools are not ethics, politics, or religion. The tools are personal courage to step into an unknown space

– to engage with deterritorialisation – which will always seem like death, the cessation of all the marks of a former life.

Vocation is therefore an event that happens to us. We cannot construct such an invitation, we can simply respond, through the ministry of others: as Ananias, as Mary in the garden. Vocation leads us to visitation from others – and then to 'baptism' (Acts 22:16). Besides being cleansed of uncritical territorialisation we can, in baptism, 'call on His name' (Acts 22:16). His call to us invited our call to Him – God invites us into a relationship of renewal and a common focussing upon 'His name' – the person and presence of Jesus – Saviour and agent of our wellbeing.

CHAPTER – 2

The Church – An Assembly of Slaves

And so, brothers and sisters, I could not speak to you as spiritual people, but rather as people of the flesh, as infants in Christ. ² I fed you with milk, not solid food, for you were not ready for solid food. Even now you are still not ready, ³ for you are still of the flesh. For as long as there is jealousy and quarreling among you, are you not of the flesh, and behaving according to human inclinations? ⁴ For when one says, "I belong to Paul," and another, "I belong to Apollos," are you not merely human?

⁵ What then is Apollos? What is Paul? Servants through whom you came to believe, as the Lord assigned to each. ⁶ I planted, Apollos watered, but God gave the growth. ⁷ So neither the one who plants nor the one who waters is anything, but only God who gives the growth. ⁸ The one who plants and the one who waters have a common purpose, and each will receive wages according to the labour of each. ⁹ For we are God's servants, working together; you are God's field, God's building.

¹⁰ According to the grace of God given to me, like a skilled master builder I laid a foundation, and someone else is building on it. Each builder must choose with care how to build on it.

1 Corinthians 3:1-10 (NRSV)

Vocation emerges from a sign – the light, the voice – illuminating and clarifying the greater purposes of God. This method provides another 'way' of reading creation and the human journey. The key is not the perfection of settlements – territorialisation: rather this divine call is accessible only outside of these kinds of walls. As civilisations give more priority to building walls of security through science, rational description, assessment and planning, globalisation becomes a term to describe the earth becoming one home. The secular view of reality as 'our planet' and 'our responsibility' to decide how best to order and secure life. One settlement, one territory: human responsibility.

Paul is called to be an apostle – sent to engage with others. He was to operate by concentrating upon strategic settlements – but the good news he brought was to unsettle, to deterritorialise, and to switch the focus from human assessment and achievement to the mystery of salvation. To make whole or holy, by divine grace, the incomplete, partial nature of human life and earthly existence. The call is to be saints – colleagues of the angels, for whom the fullest reality is to be joined in the worship of Heaven, declaring before God 'Holy, Holy, Holy' – a trinity of praise to the Trinitarian source of life and salvation.

The focus is the 'name of our Lord Jesus Christ' – we respond to His call, by calling on His name. Not through systems of ideas and institutions which will inevitably atrophy - but through the 'signs' we encounter by going into the wilderness of the open road, to be open to further moments of exchange. Our worship and prayer are attempts to step out of any sense of settlement. This is the arena in which 'all of you should be in agreement' (verse 10) – having the same mind and purpose. This call is counter-intuitive because it remains a sign, and never provides a solution in terms of particular beliefs or behaviours. Which is why the spiritual journey is presented in terms of weakness and dependency – readiness for further unveiling of the path ahead (1 Corinthians 2:3).

The important element is the Spirit working within, rather than any particular outward manifestations. In the incarnation of Jesus the flesh is subject to decay and death: the Spirit remains powerful and effective. Faith in the incarnation is faith in this spiritual process: too often it has been confused with more tangible signs of human flourishing. To be called is to recognise and then to continue to trust this inner presence and power – a manifestation of what is offered to us in 'the name of the Lord Jesus'.

Such a reality does not lead to the opposite effect – the marginalisation of the flesh and a crude puritanism which seeks special spiritual perfection. As Paul makes clear, the way of the flesh is the way of the spiritual journey. The key is to recognise the proper sources and outcomes. Hence his huge efforts to collect funds for the poor in Jerusalem. A practical, material expression of an inner call – manifested in a 'sign' to encourage not just charity, but an awareness and empathy to order more structured support as an expression of the shared love in Christ.

A second example would be Paul's teaching in 1 Corinthians 6:15-20, that the body is a temple of the Holy Spirit. Fornication is a sin, a missing of the mark, because it subjects the body to external forces as part of the economic exchange of the market – buying the body of a prostitute to seek selfish satisfaction. By contrast, Paul is clear that marriage is an act of sanctification – flesh made holy or whole in a sign that will continue to shape and to succour each party – the flesh redeemed by giving the self away to another – a picture of Christ and His Bride the Church. A transaction of gift rather than of purchase.

A similar model is presented in 1 Corinthians 8 regarding the issue of food sacrificed to idols. Paul is robust about being willing to share with all kinds of people, but clear that the fundamental approach should be restraint for the sake of the other in their need. The flesh requires signs and signals that provoke the discipline of the 'no' as well as the fruits of affirmations. The latter trajectory will always be subject to the temptations towards selfishness – settlement behind secure 'walls': the 'no' to the self will always predicate the crisis of a more complex way of relating to others and of regarding the self. This must have been the experience of Ananias in stepping out of his newly found Christian fellowship to offer himself to the one 'breathing murderous threats' – Saul the persecutor of the Way.

In each of these instances the Gospel is always a gift – a call received through grace, and a call offered in grace – in the name of the Lord Jesus. Such a vocational dynamic will always challenge the traditional sites of human settlement: the oikos or household, for the family: the polis or city for the community: the Temple for adherents of a particular religious grouping. By contrast, in Paul we find the development of the ecclesia – the assembly of those called out of household and civic or religious groups, into a space that by its very nature existed to be open to others. Echoes of the famous quote attributed to William Temple about the Church of England – when he said that the Church of England was the only club that existed for the benefit of non-members.

This inner spiritual energy – to be apostolic – offering the call to others through signs and moments in the name of the Lord Jesus – required a particular shaping. Paul uses the image of a Body in 1 Corinthians 12. A Body always subject to the Head. He began to develop orders of elders, presbyters, deacons – a hierarchy in the proper sense of that word – as the appropriate ordering of sacred or sanctifying power. Each element exercised a role and authority enabling the outflow and operation of Divine Grace – rather than the human temptation to exercise personal power. In this sense each member of the ecclesia was called to be a slave to others – within and especially going beyond that particular fellowship. The whole trajectory of every member was to be downwards – to the lowest place, the point of maximum sacrificial service. A reversal of the workings of the household or the city/community – which values seniority and oversight. Leadership is modelled by the child in the midst, as Jesus teaches in Matthew 18:1-5.

These power dynamics have been handled by theories of representation, most recently in western history through the development of democracy – whereby people vote to give their 'power' to others, to exercise on their behalf. Often democracy is presented as the apex of human maturity and achievement – despite the inevitable persistence of corruption and self-seeking. By contrast, the ecclesia of Paul is a doulocracy – a system of living-in-slavery-together – each offering the self unconditionally to the service of the body and of every other member. This is the real importance of Paul's use of this image in 1 Corinthians 12.

The ecclesia becomes an assembly of submission rather than of negotiated self-expression – which has been the model of choice from Thomas Hobbes in the seventeenth century onwards.

This model of ecclesia then becomes a creative critique of the oikos (household), the polis (community organisation) and the temple (religious cult). Each is challenged to hand over hierarchy to the purposes of sanctification in the name of the Lord Jesus, rather than assuming that hierarchy is a human tool for efficient organisation. Similarly each site of human management is challenged to operate not by seeking to promote and empower its members in ways that are best for each of them – rather the task is to invite adherents to hear the call – the light and the voice – the evocation of the spirit within, that finds the pull to fulfilment through the self-sacrificial service of others. Rooted in acknowledging dependency on 'others', especially the stranger who can become a friend.

Thus the church as ecclesia is called to a dual role. In one sense it will always be one group among many others in a particular society. The task is to try to be salt, leaven, a remnant – through creative interactivity – a generous mutuality and a courageous witness to core Christian values. This would be the recognised role of the churches in much of western society.

On the other hand, the church has a unique role in being always radically inclusive, seeking to breach boundaries and to invite others into the risk of stepping out from their settlements on to the open road where new perspectives and experiences can be received. An invitation into a doulocracy[1] not a democracy.

Endnotes

[1] Doulos is the word used in the New Testament for slave.

CHAPTER – 3

From Slavery to Adoption

There is therefore now no condemnation for those who are in Christ Jesus. ² *For the law of the Spirit of life in Christ Jesus has set you free from the law of sin and of death.* ³ *For God has done what the law, weakened by the flesh, could not do: by sending his own Son in the likeness of sinful flesh, and to deal with sin, he condemned sin in the flesh,* ⁴ *so that the just requirement of the law might be fulfilled in us, who walk not according to the flesh but according to the Spirit.* ⁵ *For those who live according to the flesh set their minds on the things of the flesh, but those who live according to the Spirit set their minds on the things of the Spirit.* ⁶ *To set the mind on the flesh is death, but to set the mind on the Spirit is life and peace.* ⁷ *For this reason the mind that is set on the flesh is hostile to God; it does not submit to God's law—indeed it cannot,* ⁸ *and those who are in the flesh cannot please God.*

⁹ *But you are not in the flesh; you are in the Spirit, since the Spirit of God dwells in you. Anyone who does not have the Spirit of Christ does not belong to him.* ¹⁰ *But if Christ is in you, though the body is dead because of sin, the Spirit is life because of righteousness.* ¹¹ *If the Spirit of him who raised Jesus from the dead dwells in you, he who raised Christ from the dead will give life to your mortal bodies also through his Spirit that dwells in you.*

¹² *So then, brothers and sisters, we are debtors, not to the flesh, to live according to the flesh—* ¹³ *for if you live according to the flesh, you will die; but if by the Spirit you put to death the deeds of the body, you will live.* ¹⁴ *For all who are led by the Spirit of God are children of God.* ¹⁵ *For you did not receive a*

spirit of slavery to fall back into fear, but you have received a spirit of adoption. When we cry, "Abba! Father!" [16] *it is that very Spirit bearing witness with our spirit that we are children of God,* [17] *and if children, then heirs, heirs of God and joint heirs with Christ—if, in fact, we suffer with him so that we may also be glorified with him.*

Romans 8:1-17 (NRSV)

In Romans 8 Paul draws a contrast between flesh and spirit, death and life. It is important to remember that 'death' is not simply a biological issue, as would be the case for secular humanism and the contemporary struggle to keep prolonging life through medical technology and more wholesome living conditions. In the light and call (voice) of the Christian Gospel, death is a spiritual state, which can occur within human life. Similarly the spiritual rebirth of Resurrection is a gift to be accepted and experienced within this life. Hence the power acknowledged in Martyrdom – as a path to true life – a vivid illustration of the way of the cross.

In this sense the Gospel of life works through a double negative. The first is the negation of the self through stepping outside of the safety of 'settlement' on to the open road and thus being exposed to the light and the voice of the call of Jesus. Spirit speaking to spirit, enabled by the negation of the self as the centre point of being. The second negation is the expression of the negated-self (slave of Christ) through putting the sacrificial service of others before one's own needs or desires. The offering of love, within the love of God. This is an enactment of a light and a voice that can connect with those being thus served – as an invitation to their own spirit to be awakened by such generosity and this desire to reciprocate – love calls to love and the outcome is love offering back to love.

St John's Gospel talks of the light and call to love God because He first loves us – in the Son, and through the gift of the Spirit.

Such a movement of love means that "you are not in the flesh; you are in the Spirit." This kind of death, this double negation, in fact enables the shift from the settlement to the open road, so that "Christ is in you" more completely (whole:holy:sanctus).

By contrast, the Roman society (with its Jewish subtext in Jerusalem and other major centres) used death as a single negation: judgement and the ending of life. The political power used crucifixion as a particularly brutal means of controlling slaves and giving a clear message about conformity to established economic hierarchies. The Jewish leaders debated about Resurrection, but could unite around death as a finalising feature of life. Some subsequent Christianity has seen life as preparation for a 'good death' to enable entry into eternity.

As F. D. Maurice showed in the nineteenth century, eternity is not a place (in the sense of a settlement forever), but a quality of relationship with the Father. In Christ we can be blessed with eternal life: as we can be sinful within our earthly condition. Paul is arguing for these spiritual realities in the first part of Romans 8. "*If Christ is in you, though the body is dead because of sin, the Spirit is life because of righteousness*" (Romans 8:10).

This truth of 'life' in its fullness through the pathway of the double negative that opens up the calling into vocation and its appropriate expression, has radical political consequences. It provides a stark challenge to the boundaried 'progress' of science, economics, politics – because these forces tend to be employed in the strictly affirmative sense. Modern liberalism asks the individual to give up the minimum 'freedom' possible in order to enable an ordered living together with other individuals. The result is continuing conflict and negotiation as each potentially autonomous individual has to decide what limits, if any, to accept to their personal freedom and lifestyle choices. Scientifically ordered rationalism becomes the key tool.

This provides a stark contrast with a call to discipline the self in order for the spirit to inflow with the Kingdom agenda (boundaryless because calling into eternity), and to enable greater sacrificial service of others. The pathways will reflect that of the Good Samaritan – the necessary systems always supplemented, and challenged to improve, by the selfless contribution of those who often engage from an outside perspective. The Christian is always in the world but not fully of the world. This fact illustrates the primary importance of signs – often fragments and moments – to which systems should ever be adjusted. In reality each 'system' survives by developing strong defence mechanisms – hence the important political and religious contribution that can be received by those who venture on to the open road.

Those on the open road become the agents of receiving a call and responding with an offering to others – as in the call of Paul and of the Good Samaritan. The outside perspective is called to contribute towards a process of restoring fragments into a greater whole – not as members recruited for conformity to what already exists, but as fellow agents of a Spirit of new life that creates salvation (health/wellbeing) for more and more people, through the Saviour (the name of Jesus). The way is one of discontinuities not consolidations. A path almost impossible for politics or religion to handle – but a way that brings a life-giving restoration to these basic endeavours.

This is not a path of reform and progress – a kind of Hegelian answer to problems. Rather this 'way' is one of Atonement: the double negative of Christ giving Himself as sign and model to others, and of His disciples giving themselves as sign and model into their particular political and religious contexts. Disciples fulfil vocation by becoming agents of vocation to those they are sent to be amongst. Such mission can operate at every level – from that of personal encounter to that of system transformation. Hence the complex of roles and structures for discipleship and church itself. The church can never be a cosy settlement – but must be always an Agent of Atonement – the vocation to a double negation through which flesh is renewed by the Spirit of holiness and wholeness. *"for if you live according to the flesh, you will die; but if by the Spirit you put to death the deeds of the body, you will live."* (Romans 8:13)

Paul proceeds by refining his understanding of doulocracy in the perspective of the vocation of the double negative: *"For all who are led by the Spirit of God are children of God. For you did not receive a spirit of slavery to fall back into fear, but you have received a spirit of adoption. When we cry, "Abba!Father!" it is that very Spirit bearing witness with our spirit that we are children of God, and if children, then heirs, heirs of God and joint heirs with Christ—if, in fact, we suffer with him so that we may also be glorified with him."* (Romans 8:14-17)

Slavery is now redefined - not as the servile state to be abolished in order to enable the freedom of the autonomous individual. Nor as a grim 'negated' life of unremitting service to others. Rather slavery – endured by Paul (*"I have made myself a slave to all"* 1 Corinthians 9:19) and by Jesus Himself (John 13:12-17: *"I, your Lord and Teacher, have washed your feet"*) becomes the means to discovering a quality of relationship with the Father, and with others in a way that turns the initial double negative into a double positive: 'love of God and love of neighbour'. This embrace into the family, each member of which can cry Abba, Father, is adoption – into a positive, life giving, Spirit filled way of being – that will be sustained by the discipline of the double negative. Yet, Paul is vividly aware of the continuing presence and power of sin, of succumbing to the temptation of the flesh – to put self first and others second.

CHAPTER – 4

Church and State – A Particular Partnership

As to the coming of our Lord Jesus Christ and our being gathered together to him, we beg you, brothers and sisters, ² not to be quickly shaken in mind or alarmed, either by spirit or by word or by letter, as though from us, to the effect that the day of the Lord is already here. ³ Let no one deceive you in any way; for that day will not come unless the rebellion comes first and the lawless one is revealed, the one destined for destruction. ⁴ He opposes and exalts himself above every so-called god or object of worship, so that he takes his seat in the temple of God, declaring himself to be God. ⁵ Do you not remember that I told you these things when I was still with you? ⁶ And you know what is now restraining him, so that he may be revealed when his time comes. ⁷ For the mystery of lawlessness is already at work, but only until the one who now restrains it is removed. ⁸ And then the lawless one will be revealed, whom the Lord Jesus will destroy with the breath of his mouth, annihilating him by the manifestation of his coming. ⁹ The coming of the lawless one is apparent in the working of Satan, who uses all power, signs, lying wonders, ¹⁰ and every kind of wicked deception for those who are perishing, because they refused to love the truth and so be saved. ¹¹ For this reason God sends them a powerful delusion, leading them to believe what is false, ¹² so that all who have not believed the truth but took pleasure in unrighteousness will be condemned.

¹³ But we must always give thanks to God for you, brothers and sisters beloved by the Lord, because God chose you as the first fruits for salvation through sanctification by the Spirit and through belief in the truth. [14] *For this purpose he called you through our proclamation of the good news, so that you may obtain the glory of our Lord Jesus Christ.* [15] *So then, brothers and sisters, stand firm and hold fast to the traditions that you were taught by us, either by word of mouth or by our letter.*

2 Thessalonians 2:1-15 (NRSV)

The double negative of the call to Christian witness can issue in positive blessing. But on its own, this contribution from the discipline and perspective of the open road has a limited effect. There is another negativising provision within the Divine economy through which slaves are adopted as children who continue to worship and serve. This is the provision for what Paul, in the second letter to the Thessalonians, calls 'the restraining' force (Katechon).

Interpreters identify the Katechon with a range of possibilities: with the Apostle himself, with the role of the church, with Christ, with the effect of the Gospel or with the work of angelic forces. But most interpreters recognise that the restraining force is the divine vocation – the light and the voice – of the state: the established political powers. Paul himself recognises the positive role of the state in Romans 13 *"Let every person be subject to the governing authorities; for there is no authority except from God, and those authorities that exist have been instituted by God."* (Romans 13:1). The peace and security brought to great swathes of the world by the Roman Empire provided the context which made Paul's journeyings across open roads and his contact with countless communities possible. Paradoxically the Imperial system of law which failed to reach a proper verdict in the trial of Jesus, but still crucified Him, also provided the context for the Gospel of His Resurrection to be spread far and wide.

The sovereign ruler is presented as an ordering, restraining force, to whom citizens should gladly pay taxes (Romans 13:7). The 'secular' state was given a theological legitimacy. Augustine developed the idea of Two Cities: the city of God and the earthly city – two dimensions within which Christians and others could live. Aquinas saw Rome as a spiritual reality, with a political role of preserving the unity of Christendom as a key notion, just when the actuality of Empire dissolved under political pressures for greater independence and autonomy. By the time of Calvin the 'restraining' force was the Christian preaching of the Gospel – a moral force in a hostile world. But the vocation of the state has remained an important factor in the West. Newman, in a lecture in 1838 stated that "there is a fierce struggle, the spirit of Antichrist attempting to rise, and the political power of those countries which are prophetically Roman, firm and vigorous in repressing it".

In the twentieth century Bonhoeffer identified it as 'the face of order' while the German legal philosopher Carl Schmitt, coming from a Roman Catholic background, recognised the Katechon as a force that not only restrains and conserves, but also creates and renews. For Schmitt there was a positive possibility from this negative root of vocation – much in the manner that Paul recognises when he balances the unremitting negativity of *"the lawless one apparent in the working of Satan"* (2 Thessalonians 2:9) with the call of disciples to provide *"the first fruits* (or the beginning) *for salvation through sanctification by the Spirit and through belief in the truth."* (2 Thessalonians 2:13).

This negation to enable first fruits highlights the importance for disciples not simply of offering challenge and correction to the political and religious institutions and systems of the time, but also to work creatively with them. Paul is clear that the lawless one apparent in the working of Satan *"uses all power, signs, lying wonders..."* (2 Thessalonians 2:9). The devil uses the same spiritual instruments as the Saviour – signs that open up new possibilities – but for the flesh rather than for the spirit. A worldly agenda well suited to secular materialistic humanism.

In this model the state can be seen as functioning by providing minimum restraint – as advocated by Hobbes and many subsequent political thinkers. The priority is to maximise the freedom of the autonomous individual. By contrast, the call – the light and the voice – of the Spirit, in the name of the Lord Jesus, seeks to maximise the negation of self, in order to enable the fuller fruition of the Body of Christ, the children adopted because of their slave like attitude and activities.

Therefore the Katechon is not simply a mechanism of government and control: rather it can be seen as a spiritual force for goodness to be called forth (vocation) in a fallen world whose temptation is always to seek the greater wellbeing of the self – the flesh as each person experiences it.

The task of restraining is not simply to control or fight evil, nor to simply manage it to minimise social disruption. Rather the task of restraining is also, and primarily, to play a political part in offering and recognising the kind of signs which highlight and encourage the possibilities of greater solidarity – closer communion with the Father, Abba, and with others as children of that same Father. The state promotes the spirit of good parenting by its openness to offer good parenting to its citizens – through institutions and systems, but more crucially, through challenging the destructive signs that seek to endorse and develop selfishness – life according to the flesh, measured by physical and material criteria.

Such a theology is realistic about the mixed currents within creation, and the complementary roles of the call to Christian discipleship through the church, and the call to political oversight through the state. Both vocations unfold through the path of a negativity that subdues fleshiness and opens the way for a deeper spirit of sanctification – the presence and purposes of God more fully in our midst.

In practice these vocations invite disciples not to be simply or primarily critical of shortcomings, but rather to especially notice signs of support, solidarity and commitment to more appropriate nourishment. Such a recognition and encouragement of the contributions already being made towards extending grace and goodness will have the effect of drawing attention to a hinterland that can be further developed, and highlight elements of affirmation that can be part of a gathering momentum through greater awareness of significant practices and current possibilities. The particular task of discipleship is to bring to such a constructive heritage and contribution of the state an awareness of the deeper meaning of such commitment – a more self-conscious awareness of the vocation, the light and the voice, that can aid recognition of the seeds of goodness and grace, and their further nourishment, and connection with a greater purpose.

This calling to the church means that her contribution is both to complement the work of the state, as Katechon and as enabler of more positive conditions and practices for human being, and to help the state and its citizens more clearly identify the greater purposes of these roles – their vocations to recognise what can be done to nourish goodness and grace and to be thankful for their part in these purposes, and for the continuing creation of seeds and leaven, the light and voice, of the Christian Gospel.

CHAPTER – 5

On Earth as in Heaven –
Slavery and Sanctity

[11] *For no one can lay any foundation other than the one that has been laid; that foundation is Jesus Christ.* [12] *Now if anyone builds on the foundation with gold, silver, precious stones, wood, hay, straw —* [13] *the work of each builder will become visible, for the Day will disclose it, because it will be revealed with fire, and the fire will test what sort of work each has done.* [14] *If what has been built on the foundation survives, the builder will receive a reward.* [15] *If the work is burned up, the builder will suffer loss; the builder will be saved, but only as through fire.*

[16] *Do you not know that you are God's temple and that God's Spirit dwells in you?* [17] *If anyone destroys God's temple, God will destroy that person. For God's temple is holy, and you are that temple.*

[18] *Do not deceive yourselves. If you think that you are wise in this age, you should become fools so that you may become wise.* [19] *For the wisdom of this world is foolishness with God. For it is written, "He catches the wise in their craftiness,"* [20] *and again, "The Lord knows the thoughts of the wise, that they are futile."*

[21] *So let no one boast about human leaders. For all things are yours,* [22] *whether Paul or Apollos or Cephas or the world or life or death or the present or the future — all belong to you,* [23] *and you belong to Christ, and Christ belongs to God.*

1 Corinthians 3:11-23 (NRSV)

In this passage Paul reflects upon the working dynamics of the call to accept the indwelling of the Holy Spirit in relation to the much more immediate constant call of the flesh for personal survival and satisfaction. He begins by recognising the 'family' connection as children of those called to the open road and its particular spirituality – in the name of the Lord Jesus. But this is never a simple, one-off process or a securely permanent position. We remain *"people of the flesh, as infants in Christ."* (1 Corinthians 3:1). The human condition and the smallness of our capacity to respond to the call – the evocation of God, means that we must be equipped for a continuing commitment to journey and to the disciplines of the double negative.

This letter is to a small, fragile group, surrounded by much stronger systems and cultural norms, and consisting of a considerable number of slaves. The letter would easily recognise their dependency and 'smallness' – the need for milk and a progression or journey to solid food. (1 Corinthians 3:2). The relapse into *"jealousy and quarrelling"* remains a constant pressure, especially the desire for settlement: 'I belong' – to Paul, to Apollos.

The key perspective is the partiality not just of any experience or perspective – but also of any contribution offered or received. The images of planting and cultivating seeds: or foundations and then construction of a building, give examples from nature and from human industrialising control of the world, that 'parts' need to be honoured and held together in a bigger picture. The key tool is not a wholistic understanding of the process or the design – rather the key is to appreciate the purpose of all of these different endeavours. Within the purpose will be a huge variety in terms of the quality of the contributions *"gold, silver, precious stones, wood, hay, straw..."* (1 Corinthians 3:12) – which will be judged according to their quality. But our concern is not this kind of judgement – necessary as it is in our age of quality control and certain standards for health and safety. Rather, God will judge from a far better informed perspective: inner life as well as outer achievements.

Our task is to recognise that God's Spirit can dwell in all of these diverse contributions. The fragments are important as part of God's greater Kingdom purposes. This act of faith will contrast with *"the wisdom of this world"* (1 Corinthians 3:19) which is often the source of futility and craftiness – i.e. narrower aims and unworthy objectives. While learning to live with such massive diversity, the confidence of disciples in a call which invites into a common and consistent journeying allows recognition of, and trust in, a promise that *"all things are yours"* (1 Corinthians 3:21) – through the miracle of the one light and the one voice. Thus Paul, shaped by the call which he experienced on the open road to Damascus, can privilege others in receiving the same call, the same Spirit *"whether Paul or Apollos or Cephas or the world or life or death or the present or the future"* (1 Corinthians 3:22) – all belong to the disciples together.

This provides a double affirmative – the confidence of belonging to God in Christ, and the confidence of belonging together in such a diverse community. There is no affirmation in terms of intellectual coherence or social cohesion – the tendency to relapse and need further nourishment remains strong – and provides a warning to every inevitable attempt to establish settlements of organisation or understanding: of institutions or theology. Such settlements become a false totality, because they are constructed within walls, as normalising boundaries. The vocational call to the journey and risk of the open road forever fractures these comfort giving defences and allows other elements to enter, strangers, new perspectives, new challenges. *"For all things are yours"* (1 Corinthians 3:21) – the key is the "all" – inclusive and pregnant with possibilities of life not yet recognised, but precious in the sight of the Father and part of His extensive and ever extending family. Spirituality cannot be bottled and traded – only consumed and spent. Authority lies not in the coherence or cohesion we can create or control – but in Christ (1 Corinthians 3:23).

This is why the spiritual life is nurtured through prayer – an opening of the imagination around the realities of fracturedness and incompletion, the call to recognise the light and the voice, and the owning of the indwelling that can grow into a faith and confidence to risk more into the sacrificial service that places us at the foot of the cross and the feet of those we encounter.

The model in scripture for this kind of 'slavery' is that of the angels, who fulfil two complementary roles. Angels are involved in contemplation of God, the mystery of prayer and worship around the throne or sovereignty of the Father. The refrain is Holy, Holy, Holy – the wonder of what is recognised in the worship of the church as Sanctus. This angelic model is a sign of the spiritual slavery that puts God at the centre. The denial of any kind of 'self' in order to be part of the corporation of praise. Satan fell because he sought a more personal agenda.

The other model provided by the angels in scripture, besides that of the centrality of Sanctus, is a specific contribution to sanctification: ministries of visitation which bring light and voice into human lives, invitations to accept more fully the sovereignty of God. The emphasis upon hierarchy through the nine ranks of angels is not a human understanding of differentiation and rising superiority. As Dionysius and Aquinas made clear, hierarchy means the ordering of sacred power. It is the structuring of God's grace into the world. Thus the different ranks of angels, focussing around the worship of Sanctus, and the ministry of visitation, are simply different expressions of the one sovereign power and purpose of the Father. Angels are one in a slave spirituality of Sanctus and sanctification – love of God and love of neighbour in the New Testament terminology of Jesus.

It is by contemplating the glory of the King and His sovereignty, that His grace can be appropriately accessed more fully on earth. The double negative of putting the self at the foot of the cross and at the feet of those we encounter beyond our defensive settlements, lays the foundation for the double affirmation through the call to Sanctus and sanctification.

The doulocracy is called to a ministry of praise and of visitation.

CHAPTER – 6

The Marks of the Church – Weakness and Folly

For the message about the cross is foolishness to those who are perishing, but to us who are being saved it is the power of God. [19] *For it is written,*

"I will destroy the wisdom of the wise,

and the discernment of the discerning I will thwart."

[20] *Where is the one who is wise? Where is the scribe? Where is the debater of this age? Has not God made foolish the wisdom of the world?* [21] *For since, in the wisdom of God, the world did not know God through wisdom, God decided, through the foolishness of our proclamation, to save those who believe.* [22] *For Jews demand signs and Greeks desire wisdom,* [23] *but we proclaim Christ crucified, a stumbling block to Jews and foolishness to Gentiles,* [24] *but to those who are the called, both Jews and Greeks, Christ the power of God and the wisdom of God.* [25] *For God's foolishness is wiser than human wisdom, and God's weakness is stronger than human strength.*

[26] *Consider your own call, brothers and sisters: not many of you were wise by human standards, not many were powerful, not many were of noble birth.* [27] *But God chose what is foolish in the world to shame the wise; God chose what is weak in the world to shame the strong;* [28] *God chose what is low and despised in the world, things that are not, to reduce to nothing things that are,* [29] *so that no one might boast in the presence of God.* [30] *He is the source of your life in Christ Jesus, who became for us wisdom from God, and righteousness and*

sanctification and redemption, [31] *in order that, as it is written, "Let the one who boasts, boast in the Lord."*

1 Corinthians 1:18-31 (NRSV)

T he flesh has a strong instinct for nurture – for affirmation. Worldly wisdom strives to provide and safeguard such nourishment – the meeting of desire and the security of settlement. By contrast, *"the message about the cross is foolishness to … the wisdom of the wise"* (1 Corinthians 1:18-19). The negative disciplines of denial and putting the self at risk on the open road seem foolish to such worldly wisdom. (Hence the example of a man who went down from Jerusalem to Jericho and was attacked by thieves who left him half dead – Luke 10:30).

There is an element of Christian spirituality which seeks to take this teaching in 1 Corinthians 1 seriously, by suggesting that the soul requires a different kind of nourishment from the flesh or bodiliness of human being, and thus a powerful tradition of asceticism has developed. The spiritual task is then identified as a call to deny the instincts of the flesh and thus make space for a more self-conscious acknowledgement of the presence of God and the priorities of the agenda of His Kingdom. This becomes an attractive spirituality because it seems to give proper emphasis to the 'spirit' and takes seriously the corrupting temptations of the flesh.

But such a reading too easily becomes a dangerous oversimplification. The good news of Jesus Christ is that the Word becomes flesh: the light that enlightens every creature given the miraculous gift of life (John 1). The gift of the Holy Spirit, in and through Jesus Christ, is not to purify the spirit by distancing that part of our being from the fleshly. This becomes the seed of Pharasaism, Puritanism, and other forms of safely separated Christian identity – a rather superior form of settlement – with strong walls to protect and discipline behaviour and belief. Rather, the mystery and the miracle which Jesus presents, and with which Paul the highly trained Pharisee wrestles, is the fact that through the indwelling of the Holy Spirit, the flesh is purified and made more whole. The kernel of the Gospel is the resurrection of the body – not it's elimination or discarding. The nourishment needed by the flesh is that of an indwelling light and voice – the call that transforms and redirects fleshliness. Paul pursued his vocation following the encounter on the open road to Damascus by remaining the same fleshly kind of person – equally energetic, passionate, combative, risk-taking – after, as before this moment of revelation and blessing.

And this reality, the transformation of the flesh, the resurrection of the body, through the visitation and call of the Spirit – the name of Jesus, is good news for the whole world. Salvation or well-being is for the world, not just for the church (John 3:17). This is the point of baptism, and the discipline of confession seeking absolution. Ownership of the necessity of the negative, of the need for washing, cleansing, renewal, is foundational to becoming open to the call of the Spirit to receive the light and the voice that provides new direction, hope and assurance. The light enlarges the possibility of vision (imagination as well as observation). The voice is the refinement of conscience (intuition as well as a sense of recognisable assessment).

This is why those who are first called to model ecclesia in the shape of the Gospel are 'weak' and 'foolish' in the eyes of the world – a doulocracy: *"Consider your own call … not many of you were wise according to the flesh, not many were powerful, not many were of noble birth"* (1 Corinthians 1:26). In fact Paul makes clear that God chooses, calls *"things that are not, to reduce to nothing things that are"* (1 Corinthians 1:28), since Christ Jesus becomes for us *"righteousness and sanctification and redemption"* (1 Corinthians 1:30). The emphasis upon an absolute negativity – things that are not – indicates the vital importance of this discipline, not to destroy the flesh, but to open the flesh to transformation into the stuff of sanctity, righteousness and redemption. Paul uses the contrast between fornication and marriage on a number of occasions to make this point. Fornication is an undisciplined pandering to the desire of the flesh for the satisfaction of the self – within the orbit of an individual approach to reality. The small world of what can be seen and experienced by the self provides the key reference points. By contrast, marriage is based upon the discipline of the renunciation of all others, a negative to every desire for others, in order to enable concentration upon, and nourishment of, a particular call and relationship. A connectivity which becomes a sacrament, a bodily union – the sign of the faithfulness of Christ to His church, and that of His church to her Lord.

The foundational stance of Christian spirituality is to offer the self in slavery – to become something "that is not" in order to be able to be called into a new blessing of sanctity, righteousness and redemption.

This emphasis upon the priority of discipline and the negative has an important implication for theology – which frequently tends towards the temptation to say too much, to aim for settlement. The signs of Jesus retreating to the wilderness or writing in the sand are key markers of the unfolding of vocation. 'Nothing' as a supreme negative is, in the Gospel sense, an active state, a journeying into the open road, and thus a state of heightened receptivity and renewed possibility. This indicates that there is no direct line to 'knowledge' – such efforts so easily become the foolishness that Paul associates with Greek confidence in the human ability to think or reason in order to establish intellectual cohesion, and with the Jewish emphasis upon 'signs' that are captured and explained in definitive ways to provide a strong sense of spiritual settlement, strictly controlled by a self-appointing leadership.

Courage to step out on the open road, self-consciously for Paul after his Damascus Road calling, implies a willingness to hold a question mark to established certainties or settlements, and to be willing to meet further light and voice that will illuminate and call beyond current structures of thought and language. This is the revolutionary purpose of prayer – which too easily becomes domesticated, rather than being the means of undertaking this journey that prioritises the negative and places the flesh in a place of risky exposure to the unknown. The gift of indwelling comes through our willingness to be continually dispossessed of what has been given. Thus Paul writes of Jesus to the Philippians *"who, though he was in the form of God, did not regard equality with God as something to be exploited, but emptied himself, taking the form of a slave..."* (Philippians 2:6-7).

The common ground for the spiritual journey is that of the slave – placing the self totally at the call of an Other, for the sake of others.

The social, missionary dimension of this spirituality, the doulocracy, is portrayed graphically when Jesus summarises His entire ministry in Matthew 25 by saying that the test of the transformation of the flesh into the spirit of wholeness comes when disciples leave the safety and comfort of their own 'settlements' in order to descend into the sheer negativity of hunger, thirst, isolation, nakedness, sickness or imprisonment – to visit and offer the self into such challenges. To own their debts to these needs in others. The journey into such encounters risks the openness of a road not yet marked with familiar systems of sustenance and care (settlements) and the first stage of this journeying is that of the encounter – and the enriching of wholeness or sanctification for all involved. There may well be schemes for addressing such challenges more systematically and inclusively – the ways of politics and religion. Christians always have parts to play in such endeavours – but the primary call is to risk the initial encounter and the foundational connectivity between the Father and all of His children – tested and worked through by means of establishing the initial solidarity of the doulocracy.

In this way *"the cross of Christ might not be emptied of its power"* (1 Corinthians 1:17) – but rather becomes the template for laying down life for others – that spirituality of the double negative (put God and neighbours before self) to enable the vocational call to a double positive (love God and neighbour as self). Such an understanding of the cross provides an important challenge to any notions of personal salvation. The brokers of salvation in the name of Jesus Christ are slaves – the poor and needy and those who identify through such negativity to a willingness to receive a different, renewing, including light and voice. This is a devastating critique of worldly power – the promotion of the flesh: and an invitation to be open to visitation by a different power – that of the Spirit of Holiness, the name of the Lord Jesus, the presence of the Father.

CHAPTER – 7

Ecclesia – Workshop of Salvation

However that may be, let each of you lead the life that the Lord has assigned, to which God called you. This is my rule in all the churches. Was anyone at the time of his call already circumcised? Let him not seek to remove the marks of circumcision. Was anyone at the time of his call uncircumcised? Let him not seek circumcision. Circumcision is nothing, and uncircumcision is nothing; but obeying the commandments of God is everything. Let each of you remain in the condition in which you were called.

Were you a slave when called? Do not be concerned about it. Even if you can gain your freedom, make use of your present condition now more than ever. For whoever was called in the Lord as a slave is a freed person belonging to the Lord, just as whoever was free when called is a slave of Christ.

1 Corinthians 7:17-22 (NRSV)

The New Testament word ecclesia (Ekklesia) is related to the term translated as calling – Klesis. This is a very particular kind of calling, and of gathering.

In the nineteenth century F. D. Maurice identified the conditions necessary for being open to Divine Truth – as a challenge to those who believed that the key was simply focussed upon reading Scripture or observing tradition. The conditions included:

First a continuous waiting for light in a spirituality of attention.

Second, a distrust of normal assumptions: a hermeneutic of suspicion in more modern language.

Third a readiness to be detected in error: the grounding in repentance or metanoia that owns the human tendency to pay more attention to apparently graspable agenda, rather than owning the need for correction and future development.

Fourth, Maurice emphasised the crucial ownership of the fact that God's meaning is infinitely larger than human capabilities, and thus challenges any sense of ownership of the small, partial nature of human experience and understanding.

Finally, a joyful acceptance that others may perceive an aspect of truth which has not been noticed in a particular context or set of experiences.

These 'conditions' not only provide a framework for each follower 'called' into discipleship, more importantly, they provide the tools for the working of a gathered Christian community – the ecclesia.

This reality explains why the New Testament has a huge range of images for the church – but no set definition. Evocative terms include salt of the earth, a letter from Christ, a net, a vineyard, a building on the rock. While Jesus used the collecting term kingdom to indicate an ever including movement, Paul chose to deploy the word ecclesia to point towards more focussed gatherings called to be agents of this incoming kingdom. Members of a movement caught up in an outpouring of the sanctifying spirit for the salvation of the world.

To emphasise the complexity, dynamism and mutuality of this developing organisation Paul used the metaphor of a Body. The more technical organisational term was ecclesia.

In secular Greek ecclesia referred to an assembly convened in a 'city' (which could be quite a small community). Often the 'representatives' who attended were heads of households, full citizens. For Paul baptism conferred full citizenship in the household of faith – abolishing localised domestic, economic and political hierarchies to establish a radical inclusiveness and equality.

In the Greek secular model, the ecclesia came to a mind which was acceptable locally – in that particular context. Hence the fuss at Ephesus when the 'ecclesia' was in confusion. The task was to settle issues into an acceptable order. There was no meeting for worship, which was as, in modern times, privatised – except for the cult of the Emperor.

In 1 Corinthians 11:18-27 Paul owns this formative template: *"when you come together as ecclesia, I hear that there are schisms among you"*. The first task of the ecclesia was to discern a unifying order. But for Paul, as a Roman citizen, this was always to be within the greater order of Salvation (as opposed to that imposed politically through the Roman Imperium).

In the Gospel of Matthew there is recognition of the same dynamic, in Matthew 18:15-17. If there is a dispute it is to be explored in the ecclesia. In Matthew 16:17 the ecclesia of Jesus is to be built upon rock – the solidarity of a common foundation.

The binding force of the ecclesia, and of its place in God's greater scheme of salvation comes not through the political and institutional forces of law, but through the mystical experience of being 'in Christ'. The outer is measured and ordered by the inner. The unseen holds the key to handling the seen. Prayer will always be prior to experience or intellect.

Consultation and conversation are always more important than crudely imposed dogma or tradition.

Paul recognises in his dealings with the ecclesia forming in a number of places as a result of his teaching and ministry that the resources of reason and tradition can never fully cope with the ambiguity of human experience, the continual tensions caused by the tendency to absolutise what can only ever be partial perceptions, and the frustration of seeking short cuts to 'order' through laws and political control. Every infant Christian church was subject to these inevitable forces, and the Pauline letters give much space and attention to the issues raised.

But more important is giving priority to the miraculous gift of grace – revelation of new life in Christ. In this spiritual foundation the pressure of the particular becomes overshadowed by the sensed totality of a greater possibility – the power of hope, faith and love (1 Corinthians 13).

The focus on Christ enables eternity to emerge from worldliness: the process of the word embracing, invading and inhabiting the flesh.

Bishop Butler challenged an increasingly confident age of Enlightenment by stressing that humankind was by nature an unformed, unfinished creature, living in the presence of a power capable of supplying these sensed potentialities, always within the framework of community. Such potential can never be captured by the individual, nor by the laws and structures continually designed to handle the unexpected and the tensions that the call of fuller formation demands.

Too much energy can be given to the short term analysis that continually categorises tensions and conflicts into the

distinction made famous by Carl Schmitt: friend or enemy –
"I am for Paul, for Apollos..." The genius of the ecclesia was
the appeal to a workshop or working space, to discern
appropriate ordering as lives unfolding, developing, colliding
and struggling to evaluate or discern the future. This gathering
was always locally sensitive – but for Paul, the foundation and
formation of being 'in Christ' enabled every diverse branch or
part to be recognised positively as part of a Body – each subject
to One Head: a common Lord and Master.

The resources could never simply be law – but always law
subject to the correction and enlargement of grace. Prayer
became the common discipline to open the many to the
enfolding grace of the One. This way of workshop did not
involve a withdrawal from the tensions and complexities of the
world, but rather a working with them in a spirit of trusting
hope and love. This is the engagement of the slave – slave to
the One (the Father) and slave to the many (the others). The
ecclesia works through citizens transformed 'in Christ' into a
doulocracy: a totally different energy and commitment to
transform this workshop into an agency of salvation – locally
and as a responsible part of a universal church.

For a carpenter the workshop is the place where different
pieces of wood are transformed into the stuff of new life. An
image resonant for Jesus as much as for Paul the tentmaker. In
more recent terms the process of ecclesia is described eloquently
by J. H. Newman:

> "By trying to love our ... friends, by submitting to their wishes,
> though contrary to our own, by bearing with their infirmities, by
> overcoming their occasional waywardness by kindness, by dwelling
> on their excellences... we form in our hearts that root of charity,

which, though small at first, may, like the mustard seed, at last even overshadow the earth."[1]

Oscar Romero called this approach to spiritual formation "thinking with the church". Joining in a workshop to seek salvation through receiving the gift of grace 'in Christ'. Such an approach does not minimise the importance of the ecclesia as institution. It will only function with recognisable leadership, procedures and values. 'Thinking with the church' provides a corporate holding framework for individuals within a local ecclesia, and for assemblies within the universal ecclesia summoned to be built upon the rock – the solid foundation of Christ crucified and raised up. The old embracing discipline of negation and affirmation – the slavery of salvation.

Endnotes

[1] Parochial and Plain Sermons Vol 2, 1868, p.52.

CHAPTER – 8

The Pattern –
A Plurality of Possibilities

What then are we to say was gained by Abraham, our ancestor according to the flesh? ² For if Abraham was justified by works, he has something to boast about, but not before God. ³ For what does the scripture say? "Abraham believed God, and it was reckoned to him as righteousness." ⁴ Now to one who works, wages are not reckoned as a gift but as something due. ⁵ But to one who without works trusts him who justifies the ungodly, such faith is reckoned as righteousness. ⁶ So also David speaks of the blessedness of those to whom God reckons righteousness apart from works:

⁷ "Blessed are those whose iniquities are forgiven, and whose sins are covered,⁸ blessed is the one against whom the Lord will not reckon sin."⁹ Is this blessedness, then, pronounced only on the circumcised, or also on the uncircumcised? We say, "Faith was reckoned to Abraham as righteousness."¹⁰ How then was it reckoned to him? Was it before or after he had been circumcised? It was not after, but before he was circumcised. ¹¹ He received the sign of circumcision as a seal of the righteousness that he had by faith while he was still uncircumcised. The purpose was to make him the ancestor of all who believe without being circumcised and who thus have righteousness reckoned to them, ¹² and likewise the ancestor of the circumcised who are not only circumcised but who also follow the example of the faith that our ancestor Abraham had before he was circumcised.

13 For the promise that he would inherit the world did not come to Abraham or to his descendants through the law but through the righteousness of faith. 14 If it is the adherents of the law who are to be the heirs, faith is null and the promise is void. 15 For the law brings wrath; but where there is no law, neither is there violation.

16 For this reason it depends on faith, in order that the promise may rest on grace and be guaranteed to all his descendants, not only to the adherents of the law but also to those who share the faith of Abraham (for he is the father of all of us, 17 as it is written, "I have made you the father of many nations")— in the presence of the God in whom he believed, who gives life to the dead and calls into existence the things that do not exist. 18 Hoping against hope, he believed that he would become "the father of many nations," according to what was said, "So numerous shall your descendants be." 19 He did not weaken in faith when he considered his own body, which was already as good as dead (for he was about a hundred years old), or when he considered the barrenness of Sarah's womb. 20 No distrust made him waver concerning the promise of God, but he grew strong in his faith as he gave glory to God, 21 being fully convinced that God was able to do what he had promised. 22 Therefore his faith "was reckoned to him as righteousness." 23 Now the words, "it was reckoned to him," were written not for his sake alone, 24 but for ours also. It will be reckoned to us who believe in him who raised Jesus our Lord from the dead, 25 who was handed over to death for our trespasses and was raised for our justification.

Romans 4 (NRSV)

In Romans 4, with regard to Abraham, Paul writes of *"the God in whom he believed, who gives life to the dead and calls into existence the things that do not exist."* (Romans 4:17). Trust in the process of the cross – the reality of the absolute negativity of 'the dead', which can be the foundation of the "calling into existence (of) the things that do not exist" i.e. the foundation of a radically new life – the ultimate affirmation of the light and the voice of resurrection. This is the tautology of a 'crucified Messiah' – a God put to death in fleshliness in order to liberate the flesh for eternity. It is not an insignificant detail that the Risen Lord should break bread (Luke 24:30) and eat fish (Luke 24:42-43). Fleshliness is the stuff of new life, in this world and in the journey into eternity.

But this is not a simple process of 'evolution' from negative to positive. Rather the cross is a sign of interruption so that *"Hoping against hope"* (Romans 4:18) there can be a call into a confidence that discipleship enables the further fulfilment of *"the father of many nations"* (Romans 4:18). The flesh will forever decay, as had the body of Abraham in reaching *"about a hundred years old"* (Romans 4:19): while Sarah had long been considered to be barren – i.e. not able to bring new life into the world. These twin negatives of decay and limitation or lack are constant in human being, and assume social dimensions in the story of the sheep and the goats in Matthew 25 and the picture of the Last Judgement. The claim of the cross is the call to take the side of nothingness – the negatives of the decay and limitation of the flesh, most poignantly displayed on Calvary. This site of dying becomes, after an agonising pause for reflection and the testing of a faith that hopes beyond hope, the place of resurrection – new life in a way not easily recognised through the eyes of the flesh. Mary thinks that she is seeing the gardener (John 20:15), while Peter seems to see a bystander on the shore (John 21:7). Eyes are open but see nothing. In this state of not knowing, can come the visitation of the light and the voice – often through the ministry of others such as Ananias, or *"That disciple whom Jesus loved"* (John 21:7). The key is to trust in "the promise of God" and "the glory of God (Romans 4:20) – i.e. the voice and the light.

Disciples are called to take the side of nothingness in the slavery of the Lord, in their own slave-like service, and in the slavery experienced by the needy. From such slavery comes salvation. Identity is to be continually questioned and abandoned. The experience of Paul in being brought to the ground on the open road to Damascus remained the continually present template for sifting his own spirituality and that of others being called with him into the ever expanding ecclesia. In his introduction to the letter to the Romans Paul presents himself as "*a servant of Jesus Christ, called to be an apostle, set apart for the gospel of God*" (Romans 1:1). This slavery is to challenge "*ungodliness and wickedness*" (Romans 1:18) and the notion of law which copes with such realities by means of the Katechon of attempted restraining, without seeking the grace and call of the God who desires to transform such decay and limitation into the stuff of eternity itself. The law has been a 'pedagogue until the coming of Christ' (Galatians 3:24) but the advent of a call to shift out of such flesh-focussed settlements has created a new agenda and new possibilities.

The path of this new covenant or spiritual relationship and journey is that enacted through Paul himself on the open road from Jerusalem to Damascus. There is a movement through five stages – which together provide a framework for our spiritual response to this life giving and life changing call. These five stages become five marks for the church.

First is the willingness to risk the disorientation of stepping outside of familiar 'settlements'. Leaving Jerusalem, the centre of religious and political wisdom and stability.

Second is the dissolution of the roots that have seemed to provide an anchor and a compass. The throwing to the ground, or knocking off balance, and the darkness descending over all the wisdom and confidence hitherto assembled.

Third comes the new promise – the light and the voice: illumination and call. An inner experience of blessing and connection with the deeper currents of the will of the Creator. Not to obliterate the roots of what has been received so far, but to re-frame these gifts in a more radical way. The shift towards a willing embrace of slavery rather than confident superiority.

Fourth comes receiving the ministry of others – in Paul's case from the 'enemy' Ananias – with humility and attention. Ananias offered light and voice: an opening of Paul's eyes and a word calling him to be cleansed and renewed in baptism.

Fifthly, and finally, Paul is now equipped to stand up and begin a new journey, which includes revisiting his rooted 'settlements' of Jerusalem and Damascus – but more significantly, involves a continuing call across open roads to bring a similar process of disruption and the call of new life to other settlements too: both Jewish and Gentile.

This process is a repetition of the call of Abraham which forms the background to Romans 4. The willingness to leave Ur, his settlement; the dissolution of the roots of family and religion; the new encounter with the light and voice of God; the receiving of ministry from others, especially the stranger Melchizedek; and the confidence to continue journeying for the sake of a Gospel of continuing challenge and inclusion – to be the Father of many nations. (Genesis 17:4-5: Romans 4:17-18).

This journey of faith, is not a rational transaction within the framework of human systems, as Paul recognises by his allusion to the normative transaction of receiving wages for work done (Romans 4:4). *"But to one who without works trusts him who justifies the ungodly, such faith is reckoned as righteousness.* (Romans 4:5). This was the experience of Paul himself – the apparently 'godly' person, at least by the world's standards, challenged to accept the negativity of his actual condition – being in fact 'ungodly' – without a true spiritual relationship, until he was called by Grace in the openness of the road to Damascus. And this experience draws out a faith that can recognise, accept and respond to such a gift. The result has radical political and social implications, because such faith is enabled to recognise that *"the promise may rest on grace and be guaranteed to all his* (Abraham's) *descendants"* (Romans 4:16). The same was to be true of all who respond to the call in the name of the Lord Jesus – entry into the spiritual process of ever expanding the family reality through the negativity of the doulocracy that can continue to enact the saving miracle of a crucified Messiah. This journey proceeds through significant moments of encounter – in the journey of the individual through the spiritual discipline of a prayer life that ever steps outside the boundaried security of 'settlement', and through political action emanating from the engagement of when 'I saw you hungry or thirsty or a stranger or naked or sick or in prison' (Matthew 25:37-39). Such moments should create a momentum – the continuing call and challenge of a love that will ever overflow earthly endeavours and responses. For this reason prayer and worship must be at the heart of every spiritual journey – for each individual and for each community or nation. Thus there has to be acknowledgement of the fact that the creation continues to 'groan' (Romans 8:19-25) because of a desire for liberation and the struggles with false slavery: slavery that is economic or political, in the merely earthly sense.

The spiritual journey recognises the reality of labour pains, and trusts the promise of the safe delivery of new life. In describing this *"hoping against hope"* (Romans 4:18) Paul uses a word, elpis (Greek) which does not just mean a feeling that things could be better, a psychological hope. Rather this word means an effort or engagement to seek a new possibility. This dynamism is clear in the words after the naming of the groaning and the labour pains which constitute the spiritual journey, when Paul states *"For in hope we were saved. Now hope that is seen is not hope. For who hopes for what is seen? 25 But if we hope for what we do not see, we wait for it with patience."* (Romans 8:24-25). Such 'waiting' is not passive abandon but the active taking seriously of a negativity that can be pregnant with the power and purposes of God. Waiting in this sense involves a 'being in' Christ (Ephesians 1:1) which is not simply sharing a common membership (the members of a static body or settlement) – nor a holy patience amidst the chaos of the world: rather the call is to participation in the sharing of action as slaves for the sake of the name of the Lord Jesus and the wellbeing of others. So Paul issues the challenge to the Galatians *"Examine yourselves to see whether you are living in the faith. Test yourselves. Do you not realize that Jesus Christ is in you?"* so that *"you may* do what is right" (Galatians 5:5-8).

Such doing is *"by the name of Jesus Christ of Nazareth"* (Acts 4:10) – flesh indwelt, sanctification – *"there is salvation in no one else, for there is no other name under heaven given among mortals by which we must be saved."* (Acts 4:12). Worship is the prayerful positioning of the self into the presence of that Name, to enable and encourage action that will ever call the disciple out of established settlements into the unexpectedness of encounters on an open road. Such worship is the continuing formation of the ecclesia – the assembly of slaves: the doulocracy.

Pentecost proclaimed that this journey of prayer and action must flow through a multitude of languages and cultures. As Peter interpreted *"upon my slaves, both men and women, in those days I will pour out my Spirit; and they shall prophesy."* (Acts 2:18). Thus all who encounter this calling of the Holy Spirit should *"Repent,* (recognise the negativity needed to challenge uncritical fleshliness) *and be baptized every one of you in the name of Jesus Christ"* (Acts 2:38).

Then *"you will receive the gift of the Holy Spirit. For the promise is for you, for your children, and for all who are far away"* (Acts 2:39). The essential places of encounter will be in prayer, praise, the breaking of the bread (fraction of fleshliness in the crucified Messiah) and engagement with the needs of others. These are the places that will focus the call and generate the momentum of salvation.

From this *"one body ... one Lord, one faith ... one God and Father of all, who is above all and through all and in all."* (Ephesians 4:4-5) will ever emerge a plurality of possibilities to interrupt every building of boundaries and settlements. Equality is located in the invitation and its call to be a slave: the outworkings of the call will be uneven and unpredictable as further horizons emerge – a continuing invitation into openness. The cross continues to be the foundational sign of the construction of a renewed humanity. Kenosis is the model for the Christian spiritual journey. Slavery easily slides into a service valued by accomplishment – the way of the flesh. Slavery needs a constant call to identify as being part of what is not, in order to be filled with what can be. The cross continues to be the sign of the struggle of the slave in a defensive world.

CHAPTER – 9

Moments for Momentum

I appeal to you therefore, brothers and sisters, by the mercies of God, to present your bodies as a living sacrifice, holy and acceptable to God, which is your spiritual worship. ² Do not be conformed to this world, but be transformed by the renewing of your minds, so that you may discern what is the will of God—what is good and acceptable and perfect.³ For by the grace given to me I say to everyone among you not to think of yourself more highly than you ought to think, but to think with sober judgment, each according to the measure of faith that God has assigned. ⁴ For as in one body we have many members, and not all the members have the same function, ⁵ so we, who are many, are one body in Christ, and individually we are members one of another. ⁶ We have gifts that differ according to the grace given to us: prophecy, in proportion to faith; ⁷ ministry, in ministering; the teacher, in teaching; ⁸ the exhorter, in exhortation; the giver, in generosity; the leader, in diligence; the compassionate, in cheerfulness.

⁹ Let love be genuine; hate what is evil, hold fast to what is good; ¹⁰ love one another with mutual affection; outdo one another in showing honor. ¹¹ Do not lag in zeal, be ardent in spirit, serve the Lord. ¹² Rejoice in hope, be patient in suffering, persevere in prayer. ¹³ Contribute to the needs of the saints; extend hospitality to strangers.

¹⁴ Bless those who persecute you; bless and do not curse them. ¹⁵ Rejoice with those who rejoice, weep with those who weep. ¹⁶ Live in harmony with one another; do not be haughty, but associate with the lowly; do not claim to be wiser than you are. [17] *Do not repay anyone evil for evil, but take thought for what is noble in the sight of all.* [18] *If it is possible, so far as it depends on you, live peaceably with all.* [19] *Beloved, never avenge yourselves, but leave room for the wrath of God; for it is written, "Vengeance is mine, I will repay, says the Lord."* [20] *No, "if your enemies are hungry, feed them; if they are thirsty, give them something to drink; for by doing this you will heap burning coals on their heads."* [21] *Do not be overcome by evil, but overcome evil with good.*

Romans 12 (NRSV)

The summation of Paul's appeal and rendering of the Good News of Jesus Christ is proclaimed in Romans 12. An appeal to 'brothers and sisters' or a sense of family: 'through the mercies of God" – the active, continuing grace filled moments and momentum given by the Father – 'to present your bodies (fleshliness) as a living sacrifice' – the attitude and action of the slave: *"holy and acceptable to God, which is your spiritual worship"*– into sanctification through the offering of prayers.

This entrance into the 'doulocracy' undermines any attempt to conform to the current age or contemporary worldliness, and rather opens up the path of transformation *"by the renewing of your minds, so that you may discern what is the will of God – what is good and acceptable and perfect"*. The light and voice of this spiritual encounter illuminates the mind and directs action into the agenda of the Kingdom.

But, having outlined this theology and practice of the double negative – slavery to the Father and to the needs of His children, as the means to the double affirmation – love God and love neighbour as self, Paul immediately reiterates the power of the pull towards the fleshliness of the self – seeking to be thought highly of, to be raised up. In fact each had a precious part to play in the 'one body' which has 'many members' – but that part will be one of slave - like service. Too easily vocations such as prophecy, ministry, teaching, encouraging, giving, leading, caring – become a badge of identity and provide an easy affirmation of the self as this 'part' – rather than being the direction of a particular journey of sacrificial service to God and to others. These temptations mislead the individual Christian, and particular groups that seek a kind of assurance that their call is genuine and being properly performed. The accent slides to performance and its management – just as the tendency of church's under pressure manifests itself in a temptation to talk about and concentrate on 'mission' – i.e. actions and attitudes aimed at enhancing the institution rather than the slave-like prioritising of the every need of the genuinely other. The church too easily assumes the indebtedness to herself of those outside. In fact the ecclesia forms and constantly re-forms around seeking to own its slave-like debt to others, especially to those in need.

The antidote to this temptation and tendency is love that is 'genuine', a proper 'mutual affection' which involves recognising the call to 'outdo one another in sharing honour' (the art of the slave). The approach involves zeal, an ardent spirit and a focus upon serving the Lord. The markers are hope, even in suffering (against hope) and perseverance in prayer - issuing in contribution to the needs of the saints and the extending of hospitality to strangers.

Even the fruits of fellowship in this Gospel need to be held in check by yet another reminder "*do not be haughty, but associate with the lowly*" (Romans 12:16). Paul has been thrown off his balance on the open road to Damascus. He had been thrown to the ground – the lowest place. A world turned upside down.

After the space for reflection and the receipt of the ministry of his erstwhile enemy, Ananias the follower of the Way – Paul had learned that *"if your enemies are hungry, feed them; if they are thirsty, give them something to drink"* (Romans 12:20). This is a radical clarification of the Last Judgement given by Jesus in Matthew 25 – where these basic needs are enough to call out our slave-like response to the will of the Father (or King) and the struggles of His as yet unencountered children. Clearly these actions of the doulocracy, the faithful disciples, are not the means of delivering salvation or wellbeing in its entirety or completion. These attitudes and actions of faithful slaves are ways of offering those moments of encounter through which others can be thrown off balance by the light and the voice of the Gospel of the Lord Jesus. They might contribute to a change of direction, a new attitude towards the temptations to settlement, and a new desire to risk further journeying on such a radically more 'open' road.

However these are means of developing moments into the momentum of the spiritual journey enacted by Jesus, followed by Paul and proclaimed at Pentecost. As a Jew concerned with results and outcomes, Paul could not let go of a concern for judgement – the definitive evaluation of spiritual journeying and slave-like service to the Father and His children. In Romans 12 he owns that *"I will repay, says the Lord"* (Romans 12:19). False or hypocritical journeying, the constant reassertion of the flesh on its own terms, will attract 'vengeance' from God. It is not for disciples to judge – but simply to risk the journey of openness to love and its mysterious power to cleanse, renew, transform, connect – and ever to repeat such a life-giving process amidst the continuing challenges and contradictions of the earthly world.

Paul has explored this perspective more fully in Romans 2 *"Therefore you have no excuse, whoever you are, when you judge others; for in passing judgment on another you condemn yourself, because you, the judge, are doing the very same things."* (Romans 2:1). We are all subject to the frailties of the flesh – Jews and Gentiles: religious and pagan peoples – this is a key theme in the whole letter to the Romans. Disciples must recognise the smallness of the perspective or experience of any one part of the body: there needs to be trust in the presence and power of the Father – for each person and group, in others who are not of such a flock (John 10) and in the processes of failure and forgiveness – sin, repentance, redemption, righteousness. Disciples are to inhabit these journeyings with humility and wonder – and resist the temptation to establish the false securities of boundaries that seem to settle, but generally tend to throw shadows and restrict conversation – i.e. to limit the sharing of the light and the voice.

The Gospel rests on the fact that *"God shows no partiality"* (Romans 2:11): God has provided the Katechon of the state, of political and religious organisations that can offer appropriate 'restraining' as a means of providing from this first negative, a platform for a positive confidence in hearing and responding to the call of Grace. *"Live in harmony with one another; do not be haughty, but associate with the lowly; do not claim to be wiser than you are."* (Romans 12:16). These are the marks of doulocracy – the spiritual path of all who are called to be agents of the Father's Kingdom, in the name of the Lord Jesus, through the power and purpose of His life-giving Spirit.

CHAPTER – 10

From Settlement to Journey

Now it is not necessary for me to write you about the ministry to the saints, *² for I know your eagerness, which is the subject of my boasting about you to the people of Macedonia, saying that Achaia has been ready since last year; and your zeal has stirred up most of them.* *³ But I am sending the brothers in order that our boasting about you may not prove to have been empty in this case, so that you may be ready, as I said you would be;* *⁴ otherwise, if some Macedonians come with me and find that you are not ready, we would be humiliated—to say nothing of you—in this undertaking.* *⁵ So I thought it necessary to urge the brothers to go on ahead to you, and arrange in advance for this bountiful gift that you have promised, so that it may be ready as a voluntary gift and not as an extortion.*

⁶ The point is this: the one who sows sparingly will also reap sparingly, and the one who sows bountifully will also reap bountifully. *⁷ Each of you must give as you have made up your mind, not reluctantly or under compulsion, for God loves a cheerful giver.* *⁸ And God is able to provide you with every blessing in abundance, so that by always having enough of everything, you may share abundantly in every good work.* *⁹ As it is written,*

"He scatters abroad, he gives to the poor;

his righteousness endures forever."

¹⁰ He who supplies seed to the sower and bread for food will supply and multiply your seed for sowing and increase the harvest of your righteousness.

¹¹ You will be enriched in every way for your great generosity, which will produce thanksgiving to God through us; ¹² for the rendering of this ministry not only supplies the needs of the saints but also overflows with many thanksgivings to God. ¹³ Through the testing of this ministry you glorify God by your obedience to the confession of the gospel of Christ and by the generosity of your sharing with them and with all others, ¹⁴ while they long for you and pray for you because of the surpassing grace of God that he has given you. ¹⁵ Thanks be to God for his indescribable gift!

2 Corinthians 9 (NRSV)

The Church, by its very nature as an institution, has tended to take its markers from what has been identified as the process of settlement or territorialisation. An inevitable instinct to solidify identity and purpose around core, commonly recognised beliefs and patterns of behaviour. This provides Good News which, throughout human history, people have been glad to receive. The continuing pressure of the uncertainty and unevenness of human living makes the human heart long for the security and stability that such settlement brings. Jesus worked within and endorsed these kind of frameworks, as did Paul in his energetic endeavours to establish what can be recognised as 'house churches' alongside the existing structures of synagogue and Temple. This seemed to model the method of Jesus in establishing a number of interlocking 'communities', such as the twelve, the seventy, the women, while continuing to engage with the existing structures for spiritual life and its reflective outworkings, such as the Temple and the Synagogue.

The challenge, and the continuing problem, for 'churches' is the understandable tendency to focus upon such a readily acceptable form of Good News in the midst of the fragility of human life. Settlement becomes the method and the goal for spiritual life. But when the teaching and example of Jesus, and of Paul, is examined more closely, settlement is always a first, and temporary stage of the mission of God.

As Jesus enabled countless encounters with people facing all kinds of challenges and dilemmas, He affirmed the seeking of greater clarity and confidence in their sense of call, both as individuals and as various groupings, but He was always *"going on to the next village"*– to another encounter. And the real effect of His engagement was always that of unsettlement, disruption, openness to the richer experience of the wholeness and holiness of God. His crucifixion as Messiah provides the clearest indication that the fraction of every experience of fleshliness is part of the process whereby resurrection is received and blessed. His risen appearances continue this pattern of disruption and unsettlement, as does His Ascension where some doubted (Matthew 28:16-20). The journeying of the spiritual life was to continue.

This was the trajectory Paul encountered on the open road to Damascus. The first great builder of the church, the champion of the foundations being firmly in Jesus Christ, was formed by being thrown off balance, in order to receive a further challenge and call from God's presence and purpose. The church needs to learn always to live by such discipline. To be glad of settlement (Just as Jerusalem and Damascus were so precious and important to Paul) but to be willing always to venture into the unknown – where encounter with the Lord Jesus, and with His children, can be enhanced by receiving a new light and a new voice. The church, like the synagogue and the Temple, is always liable to the temptation to domesticate God's glory and grace – to seek settlement. The Gospel is given to the church, for the world, as light and voice that ever reveals the greater power and purposes of God.

The marks of the church are not simply to be one, holy, catholic, an apostolic. These four characteristics provide the dynamic of an overarching Oneness of God, the ever greater wholeness or holiness which the Spirit strives to bring, the universal scope of this mission, and the role of disciples to be agents of such good news. In this sense the marks of the church must be formed in the courage to ever break the walls of what must be 'temporary' settlements, to risk new encounters with God and His goodness. The results should always 'throw' discipleship, and call us simply to greater dependency – to the doulocracy that is the spirituality of salvation for the world.

Paul sought to institutionalise this openness to being 'thrown' by encouraging his assemblies to be 'workshops' rather than narrowly formalised gatherings. This continuing openness to the flexibility needed to embrace cultural diversity and a challenging variety of experiences made him vulnerable – both as a Christian leader with a public role seeking to link 'churches', and as a politically suspect citizen seen to be open to cross boundaries and mingling new perspectives 'in Christ'.

Thus his 'journeying' is seen as a manifestation of having no place to be home (Philippians 3:20), and someone who could be an outsider and an insider at the same time – thus in Galatians 4:12 he is seen to live like a Gentile but think like a Jew. In Corinth he displays a desire to seek flexibility in relation to the context of clashing values about sacrifice and food, while in Romans 9-11 he proclaims his continuing attachment to those who do not share his theological convictions. He is willing to cross boundaries, but refrains from invading anyone else's sense of 'territory' (2 Corinthians 10:12-18).

Thus Paul sees the ecclesia as a forum and a workshop for 'intense associations': a space for exploration emanating from a priority of desiring the stranger to feel at home. Belonging is in Christ, not in a sense of ethne or group identity (Galatians 3:14). A powerful echo of Our Lord's command to take good news to all ethnes (Matthew 28). He resists the political temptation to create a neat synthesis but seeks a continual awareness of the Gaze of God – His presence in Christ as the light that lightens every creature. The inner bonding of the Spirit is richer than any particular outward expression. There is no strategy of universalizing generalisations, but rather a continuing call to recognise and own an equality of fellowship before God (Galatians 3:25).

The marks of being bound together focus on a table fellowship, consumer habits (food), sexual morality and resistance to idolatry. This approach reflects the structuring of guilds in places like Antioch, where professional, social, and religious groups found identity and solidarity. But Paul never let a single group rest in this guild mentality. His letters bear witness to a constant need to break open defensive, restrictive and excluding views and practices – the shift towards mastery. Slaves in the doulocracy should always remain open to new agendas and commissions from their Lord and Master.

As the New Testament scholar James D. G. Dunn remarks, Paul and other leaders in the early church "recognised the validity of different forms of the gospel in different contexts…and had agreed not to try to preach or enforce their understanding in the other's contexts."[1] The acknowledgement and acceptance by the leaders and overseers of localised churches was an expression of the working nature of the gospel enterprise at every level of organisation and witness. Thus, in the case of the famous difference between Peter and Paul at Antioch, the former as leader of the Jerusalem church, gives way to the authority of Paul in his own Gentile setting (Galatians 2:1-14). There is a mutual recognition of appropriate, but very different, oversight and the resulting expression of Christian identity.

The one ground of clear solidarity and connection between this vibrant plurality of assemblies was Paul's collection for the poor in Jerusalem. Clearly the materiality of the gospel in being particularly expressed through owning one's debts to others, was the primary tool for illustrating the way of journeying together through differences, but with a common, connected outreach of love for the neighbour in need. What was the primary connecting foundation of each assembly/workshop was to fulfil the same role in shaping the 'church' worldwide – as an international institution. Such an 'economic' expression of the kingdom project of Jesus Himself is expressed in the parable of the sheep and the goats (Matthew 25).

The 'base' in terms of needs is the clue to a 'base' spirituality that emerges by taking the lowest place and looking up to others. Assemblies as workshops operate by mingling ethnes or groups – just as Jesus exemplified to His disciples at the Last Supper with a fellowship meal that included Judas. Such a challenging and disruptive factor is a key element in the command to 'Do this in remembrance of Me'. The sharing involves a costly sacrifice for the sake of inclusiveness – to which both Peter and Judas showed marks of resistance. The working element of the 'workshop' has to be continually rededicated to a costly including invitation and embrace.

This emphasis upon a continuing openness to journeying into an unknown calling, by being thrown off balance brings challenge to every kind of organisational or cultic 'harmony' when it becomes associated with fixed marks or positions.

For Paul the collection for the needy in Jerusalem was not simply a feature of his own journeying – a common message to all the different assemblies/workshops with which he engaged. Nor was it just a pooling of resources for a worthy cause. The way in which this invitation formed such a key part of his apostleship shows that for Paul participation in the collection of funds was in fact a participation in the worship of God – a sharing in Christ's generous ministry to the poor. Those who joined together in this common act of Benefaction expressed their praise to the Benefactor of all. In 1 Corinthians (16:1-4) Paul advises a weekly offering in proportion to earnings.

Paul's challenge might seem to embody the language of competition – from rival places, but in fact it was a clear call to cooperation on the journey of witnessing to the coming of the kingdom – manifestations unfolding signs of the Reign of God. It is a point worth pondering that the oneness of the Body of Christ offering this witness in a needy world was not focussed upon agreement about belief or behaviour – but was simply expressed through money – in a material enterprise. A radical enactment of responding to the recognition of owing a debt to others. Church is the joining of this response to our perpetual debt crises by the cooperation in charity of a disparate group of assemblies/workshops. The key was to equip others to make the journey, rather than to offer the illusion of some kind of earthly destination.

This contrasts powerfully with a worldly approach to philanthropy, which tends to glorify the giver, rather than the recipients in whose image the glory of the Father can be most clearly recognised.

Endnotes

[1] The Theology of Paul's letter to the Galatians, CUP. 1993. p.38.

CHAPTER – 11

Fraction as Fruitfulness

If I speak in the tongues of mortals and of angels, but do not have love, I am a noisy gong or a clanging cymbal. ² And if I have prophetic powers, and understand all mysteries and all knowledge, and if I have all faith, so as to remove mountains, but do not have love, I am nothing. ³ If I give away all my possessions, and if I hand over my body so that I may boast, but do not have love, I gain nothing.

⁴ Love is patient; love is kind; love is not envious or boastful or arrogant ⁵ or rude. It does not insist on its own way; it is not irritable or resentful; ⁶ it does not rejoice in wrongdoing, but rejoices in the truth. ⁷ It bears all things, believes all things, hopes all things, endures all things.

⁸ Love never ends. But as for prophecies, they will come to an end; as for tongues, they will cease; as for knowledge, it will come to an end. ⁹ For we know only in part, and we prophesy only in part; ¹⁰ but when the complete comes, the partial will come to an end. ¹¹ When I was a child, I spoke like a child, I thought like a child, I reasoned like a child; when I became an adult, I put an end to childish ways. ¹² For now we see in a mirror, dimly, but then we will see face to face. Now I know only in part; then I will know fully, even as I have been fully known. ¹³ And now faith, hope, and love abide, these three; and the greatest of these is love.

1 Corinthians 13 (NRSV)

The issue for a recognisable 'church' structure and institution is how to handle the inevitable messiness of the pluralism which constantly emerges from the continuing journey of discipleship. The importance of spaces which give a sense of security, identity and belonging is crucial. Jesus called recognisable groups, such as the twelve, the seventy, the women: Paul established a variety of assemblies/workshops. Yet, as explored in this text, both internal and external tensions inevitably continue to arise. The call to journey keeps breaking open any sense of settlement or territorialisation. Fraction remains the centre of every Christian gathering.

The temptation to find solutions or a working synthesis are legitimate and helpful, but must always be penultimate and open to the inclusion of those who have not yet been brought into the fold (John 10:16). An interesting picture of this uncomfortable space is offered by the philosopher Gillian Rose, who used the phrase 'the broken middle'. By this she meant the impossibility of a pure, formed position, and the recognition of the reality of the need to face continuing pressure, challenge and call for change. Yet such plurality did need an element of the institutional – not through laws, but through a commitment to participation in an ever more public conversation. The earthliness of our journeying in this life is ever drawn into the glory of the inbreaking City of God.

For Rose the 'broken middle' described an openness to engaging with the will of God and with the wills of others, while resisting the temptation to close down the conversation for the sake of supposed clarity or completeness. Hence the key role of mediation. The church is the place of this priestly work – enabling advocacy, sacrifice and service through worship that offers openness to the glory of God by owning our own utter dependence and lack of ability to see or know definitively. The priest is the overseer of the assembly that is a workshop: the wider church is the means by which High Priesthood is offered through the fullest expression and magnification of Christ's cleansing, transforming and healing presence. The outcomes are the confidence of faith and the joy of hope rightly directed. The energy for such faith and hope flows from the indwelling love of Christ that enters into human neediness, into the doulocracy.

This 'church' is a borderline activity – an exploration of a broken middle within which grace is met – by the breaking of temporary staging posts, and a courage to live within the tension between order and disorder. This is the tension of the inbreaking of the kingdom of God. Rather than the fantasy of a 'perfect way' inhabited by a chosen and clearly demarcated 'few', the ecclesia is called to be a remnant losing itself like salt in a stew – to enable moments of grace and goodness to be tasted. A practical contemporary outworking is explored in The Word on The Street.[1]

This emphasis upon interruption and a 'broken middle' is especially significant within the context of the modern administrative bureaucratic state, with a concentration upon compliance and uniformity, often masked under the badge of equality. The emergence of irregular and informal spaces within and between assemblies provides scope for a different kind of renewal, not focussed on new structures (the current tendency in institutions) but emerging from imagination which transcends established borders. The aim shifts from seeking wellbeing in the present to searching for the dynamism of becoming. The tools become signs and sacraments rather than structures.

The power of the Holy Spirit is an invisible force becoming visible through the grace and mercy of God. This invisible reality embraces far more possibilities than any particular earthly manifestation can adequately express. The role of the church, locally and universally, is to represent and act as agent of this spiritual process of the invisible being made visible: the process known theologically as incarnation – the Word becoming flesh and dwelling amongst us (John 1).

This visualisation of the invisible is the role of a mediating institution – the priestly task of the church, for disciples and for others too. The commission emerges from the call and authorisation of the Father, and is fulfilled most effectively by forging a symbolic and sacramental unity which transcends empirical divisions. There is always a counter tendency to assimilate the invisible into the visible: baptism can be seen as an example (Matthew 3:13-17). However baptism properly understood is the beginning of a spiritual journey which proceeds by body ever broken open (cleansed) in order to grow more fully in the way of Christ. As the creed proclaims: "I believe in One God, the Father Almighty, Maker of heaven and earth, and of all things visible and invisible".

Ecclesial spirituality, the gathering of Christians at the foot of the cross, must have the robustness to make this 'founding rupture' or fraction the determining offer into the spiritual and practical lives of disciples. Often the local assembly can struggle with the political, social and economic implications of this cruciform mediation, and there is a huge tendency to absorb it into the genuinely devout lives of individual believers. This is vital preparatory work, as The Peace that Passes Understanding[2] tries to show. But on its own the result can be a spiritual journey for the individual or the small local group, which soon finds that there is a lack of the means or the insights to become mediators of "grace – through – fraction" into the needs of the wider world. Both Matthew 25 and Paul's collection for the needy in Jerusalem were invitations to express the Christian spiritual journey in the most public and material ways.

The katechon or restrainer that holds back the forces of evil can easily be mirrored by the church as she becomes an agency for containing the outpouring of God's grace, rather than a malleable conveyor of goodness shaping witness to the needs of the most indigent. A powerful form of 'ordering' is territory – and many churches define themselves by geographical identifiers – often in the name of 'service'. But the mystery of grace emerges across boundaries, in Rose's broken middle. Here is the challenge to the fundamentalist who narrowly defends boundaries and to the liberal who tries to minimise or deny them.

Paul recognised the diversity of the assemblies he called into being. He offered them a cocktail of encouragement to own their context, and critical challenge to acknowledge being part of a bigger picture. The priestly, mediating role of 'church' is to read these ingredients appropriately for an assembly or for a grouping of assemblies – since it is by helping Christians locally and universally to recognise and work with the tensions of human limitation, selfishness and need for security not just within the individual believer, but within each fellowship, and in the broken middle between fellowships. Ecclesia always operates as workshop.

A modern term for such a working set of institutional arrangements would be 'creative solidarity', predicated in a faith that recognised the impossibility (yet real temptation) of formed positions, and a willingness to respond to the trespasses and struggles of those who too often present as strangers. The medium of operation is godly conversation – in prayer and worship, in sharing what Charles Gore termed 'independent testimonies' and in being committed to accepting fraction as a means of receiving new life – through new tangible bodily experience.

In this sense the church is not about 'community', which quickly seeks visible marks of common understanding and practice – inevitably measured by human markers, and therefore localised and limited. Rather, the church as mediator of new life through the mysterious gift of fraction is primarily in the business of identity. Paul consistently uses the term 'in Christ'. This new identity provides the ground, the grace and the means of cooperation and connection in one Body – a Body manifested on a cross (the ultimate advertisement of slave status) and continually manifest in the sacraments that cleanse and nourish Christians for the journeying that this spirituality demands.

Ecclesia, locally and universally, is made and re-made around moments of cleansing, fraction/feeding and renewal in grace. We, though many, are one Body. The task and the challenge is to recognise this truth and pursue it. Such cohesion is primarily liturgical rather than institutional. The latter is important to provide a framework that enables practical expressions of faith, but all such witness must flow from accepting the call that throws the balance and creates complete dependency upon the grace of God – the base position of a slave.

From this liturgical grounding and re-grounding comes proclamation of this good news through word and deed. Such proclamation will own and develop marks of concreteness (tradition) to enable it to be understood and received. When Paul visited Jerusalem he acknowledged the importance of seeking the blessing of the original Apostles, and of an essential coherence about the faith entrusted to the church.

This coherence and common life was expressed in two key ways. A continuing fellowship in prayer. Paul rejoiced in, and appealed to, invisible networks of prayer that enabled churches to overcome distance and difference (2 Corinthians 1:10-11), and rooted them together in the bond of love (Philippians 1:3-4). Just as Jesus gave His motley crew of followers, sympathisers and opponents a single word: Abba, Father. Paul explores this given commonness in his exposition about the Spirit bearing witness with our spirits that we are children of God (Romans 8:15,27-28 or again in 1 Thessalonians 5:17-18). It is by prayer that each Christian is united to God and to others.

The second key connection between Christians in an ecclesia, and between churches being joined together in a common life in Christ, was expressed through the pooling of resources in the collection for the needy in Jerusalem. The practical outpouring of the love of God to honour the priorities and policies of His inbreaking kingdom.

Worship and charity are the key factors enabling and defining Christian connectivity: the manifestation on earth of the One Body of Christ – the Saviour of the world.

Such corporate solidarity depends upon, and emerges from self-giving love. The kenosis of Jesus Christ into which sacramental worship and practical charity draw the Christian believer and the ecclesia. Most powerfully expressed in Paul's great hymn of love in 1 Corinthians 13. This is the pattern for the church as well as for each disciple.

The need for clear thinking and a credible articulation of Christian views and values will be always a primary part of Christian witness and the life of the church at every level. But unlike the previous marks of ecclesia, such expressions must always be open to fraction. In 2 Corinthians 10:4-5 Paul says in literal translation *"I destroy buildings of thought"*. But, as the cross reminds us, such destruction of the Word is paradoxically the means of the Word bringing new and fuller life. The key role of the church is not to resist such testing callings, but to help interpret them for believers in the light of what Paul calls the folly of the cross. This will always be a counter cultural task, challenging the continuing temptation to retreat into safer spaces of clear understanding and regulative practice.

This is the meaning of Paul's challenge to the extremely sophisticated religion of his people – that circumcision is to be of the heart, not simply an outward ritual (Romans 2:25-29). The covenant which binds Christians across a plurality of assemblies/workshops is a promise that trusting in this invisible bond is a surer ground for hope than the trappings of outward institutional conformity.

The key connecting and holding mechanism for growth on the journey into wholeness is the new covenant, given in Christ, which provides not just a frame, but a continuing source of encouragement into new and fuller life. The whole challenge put to Nicodemus, unless a person be born of water and the Spirit (John 3:5-8). Covenant is this sense brings together both binding and promising – two active processes of settlement and deterritorialisation, of security and call to go beyond current boundaries.

Covenant offers a space for gathering and for growing – a dynamic of contradictory tensions from which the grace of God constantly emerges. This is the spirit of formation that indwells individuals and church as institution. The gathering and the growth are always for the welfare of others, not to pronounce definitively on their actions or opinions. The covenant is a connection in Love.

The folly of the cross is that such truth is enacted, never captured in political structures or religious rituals. There is One Lord, One Father, One Gaze that holds, loves and invites every creature. For this reason identity is a gift through the light of such an encounter, not a fixed form that the person or a group constructs for themselves. Such vision of and towards the Father is always being interrupted by the comings and goings of others. This continuing disturbance puts life constantly in the 'broken middle' of the tension between what is, and what is to come.

Too often church is formed in an institutional way by designing 'abstract' codes and expressions that seem to express universal realities. In fact the limitations of human language and understanding consistently hamper the effectiveness of such worthy endeavours. The church which understands truth as Christ offers it to us – in Himself (I am the truth: John 14:6), in silence before political and religious systems (John 18:38) and in worship (Samaritan woman: John 4:21-25) mediates a very different kind of grace. It is met in worship, in followership of Jesus, and in reticence before the temptations to grasp implications more definitively in the terms available at a particular moment in history. Truth as an attempted mastery of the Gospel, of the church or of the world, will always tend towards an idolatry that requires breaking open to allow more light to be received. Thus the marks of church will never be simple conformity to particular approaches.

Rather, for Paul, church is constituted by an event – the Resurrection of the Crucified: the gathering around sacramental moments of fraction, including the continuing breaking of the word. It is important to remember that this founding event was a sign of illegality – in the eyes of the state and in the eyes of the religious authorities the Crucified one had broken the law. This provides an important clue to the radicality of the Christian understanding of the nature and unfolding of the truth for the human journey.

This act of crucifixion is a crucial moment of differentiation: a judgement upon our usual understanding of law, of community building and of religious organisation. These recurring human endeavours tend to emphasis achievement and underplay the reality of sin, the tragedy of failure and the need for forgiveness. There is a temptation to focus on a superficial heavenliness that seeks energy and direction from faith in progress. The Event of the cross puts such a direction of travel in a radically different perspective. An ecclesia is called to be a laboratory forging temporary passports – temporary identities and systems of belief and behaviour in worldly terms – because of trust in a covenant of grace that irrupts into these useful constructs with more 'good news', measured by the response of the hitherto excluded.

This is why officers of the church were apostles and not simply disciples. They were essentially agents of this one Event.

Matthias was chosen by criteria which included not only personal experience of the preaching and ministry of Jesus, but also of the resurrection and ascension into heaven (Acts 1:23-28).

The church consists of those who are called to be faithful to this Event. Always ready to be thrown, rechallenged, remade: re-membered. This is how the Body of Christ operates. Truth is the tool for seeking to enable the gospel process of good news unfolding across boundaries, through brokenness, into an eternity of glory beyond the marks of any earthly kingdom.

The church is guardian of this mystery, and will be ever called to express it in her life. The facts of life: of death: of resurrection are not basically biological – but spiritual. Paul summaries this truth *"...it is no longer I who live, but it is Christ who lives in me."* (Galatians 2:20).

Endnotes

[1] The Word on the Street. Alastair Redfern, ISPCK 2015.

[2] The Peace that Passes Understanding. Alastair Redfern, ISPCK 2015.

CHAPTER – 12

Workshop as Worship and Witness – the Story of Salvation

They came to Philip, who was from Bethsaida in Galilee, and said to him, "Sir, we wish to see Jesus." ²² Philip went and told Andrew; then Andrew and Philip went and told Jesus. ²³ Jesus answered them, "The hour has come for the Son of Man to be glorified. ²⁴ Very truly, I tell you, unless a grain of wheat falls into the earth and dies, it remains just a single grain; but if it dies, it bears much fruit. ²⁵ Those who love their life lose it, and those who hate their life in this world will keep it for eternal life. ²⁶ Whoever serves me must follow me, and where I am, there will my servant be also. Whoever serves me, the Father will honor.

²⁷ "Now my soul is troubled. And what should I say —'Father, save me from this hour'? No, it is for this reason that I have come to this hour. ²⁸ Father, glorify your name." Then a voice came from heaven, "I have glorified it, and I will glorify it again." ²⁹ The crowd standing there heard it and said that it was thunder. Others said, "An angel has spoken to him." ³⁰ Jesus answered, "This voice has come for your sake, not for mine. ³¹ Now is the judgment of this world; now the ruler of this world will be driven out. ³² And I, when I am lifted up from the earth, will draw all people to myself." ³³ He said this to indicate the kind of death he was to die. ³⁴ The crowd answered him, "We have heard from the law that the Messiah remains forever. How can you say that the Son of Man must be lifted up? Who is this Son of Man?" ³⁵ Jesus said to them, "The light is with you for a little longer. Walk while you have the light, so that the darkness may not overtake you. If you walk in the darkness, you do not know where you are going. [36] While you have the light, believe in the light, so that you may become children of light."

After Jesus had said this, he departed and hid from them. [37] Although he had performed so many signs in their presence, they did not believe in him. [38] This was to fulfill the word spoken by the prophet Isaiah:

"Lord, who has believed our message,

and to whom has the arm of the Lord been revealed?"

[39] And so they could not believe, because Isaiah also said,

[40] "He has blinded their eyes

and hardened their heart,

so that they might not look with their eyes,

and understand with their heart and turn —

and I would heal them."

[41] Isaiah said this because he saw his glory and spoke about him. [42] Nevertheless many, even of the authorities, believed in him. But because of the Pharisees they did not confess it, for fear that they would be put out of the synagogue; [43] for they loved human glory more than the glory that comes from God.

[44] Then Jesus cried aloud: "Whoever believes in me believes not in me but in him who sent me. [45] And whoever sees me sees him who sent me. [46] I have come as light into the world, so that everyone who believes in me should not remain in the darkness. [47] I do not judge anyone who hears my words and does not keep them, for I came not to judge the world, but to save the world. [48] The one who rejects me and does not receive my word has a judge; on the last day the word that I have spoken will serve as judge, [49] for I have not spoken on my own, but the Father who sent me has himself given me a commandment about what to say and what to speak. [50] And I know that his commandment is eternal life. What I speak, therefore, I speak just as the Father has told me."

John 12:21-end (NRSV)

The church is always in a context demanding mission. The imperative is Matthew 28 where Jesus tells His followers to go and make disciples of all. The inclusivity had been given a particular style and edge in the summary Jesus gave to His entire ministry in Matthew 25 – in the parable of the sheep and the goats. This dynamic between judgement, the Father's commandment and the mission to save the 'world' is expressed most powerfully in John 12:21-end. The passage unfolds from a request by some Greeks (outsiders) to know something more fully about the 'truth'. The foundation is to be the method of the grain of wheat – self sacrificial, slave-like service which draws and inspires others into such truth. The key is *"if I be lifted up"*. But people will not easily believe this way into the truth for creation. Since human creatures, despite this sign, constantly display a tendency to concentrate upon a more immediate perspective – *"to love the praise of men rather than the praise of God"*. The issue of free will and the animal instinct for self-preservation.

The church is called to be a workshop (an ecclesia) to encourage and enable a fruitful response to this manifestation of the 'light of the world', to challenge resistance and short-sightedness, and to recognise a judgement that can bring life and renewal.

This 'truth' is complex. B. F. Westcott famously told a student who commented "Yes – I suppose there are two sides to every question…" "Two: surely not less than six! You can scarcely picture truth as less than a cube." Here is an image that captures something of the challenge to the ecclesia as the rock upon which the truth of Christ is founded.

The shaping and response of the ecclesia as a workshop for this divine commission crystallised in recognition of Jesus Christ as Lord. The term Kyrios had become part of common currency through the growth of Hellenistic religious cults. But the Lordship ascribed to Christ was not merely about ideas and values – more profoundly it acknowledged an existential leadership – an indwelling presence that gave sense and direction to followership. Jesus became a Living Lord – a presence and a power met especially in worship, which was the foundational work of the ecclesia. Meeting for the prayers and the breaking of the bread (Acts 2:43-47).

In this Lordship and leadership was made manifest an authority and a power which invited others to follow: to accept and recognise the so often uncomfortable way of the cross.

In this space of worship and ensuing witness into the wider world, there will always be a key element of paradox. Communication and responses are always 'indirect', as if through a glass darkly. Nonetheless there can be real relationship. This arena of paradox is the basic site of the workshop which came to be called 'ecclesia'. The theological statements necessary to enable engagement and participation will never be more than a frame and an indication – rooted in the important potential of the not, the negative, the unnoticed. The church must operate therefore not through statements or structures, but essentially through signs – in which God and others are both encountered in their fullness, but also, at the same time, partially – due to the context of humanity on earth being placed 'lower than the angels'. Hence the heavenward direction of the Lord's Prayer.

For Anglicans this paradoxical nature of truth and of the human journey is held in the discipline of common worship, around different theological emphases, behavioural practices and liturgical styles. The Orthodox teacher Sergius Bulgakov uses the term 'antinomy' to try to grasp this critical agenda for the ecclesia:

"an antimony simultaneously admits the truth of two contradictory, logically incompatible, but ontologically necessary assertions. An antinomy testifies to the existence of a mystery beyond which the human reason cannot penetrate. This mystery is nevertheless actualised and lived in religious experience. All fundamental dogmatic definitions are of this nature."[1]

The ecclesia is called to be a workshop where this mystery cannot be stated in words without contradictory outcomes, and yet such mystery can be actualised and lived in the experience of faith in and worship of God.

To enable this mystery unfolding through antinomy to be encountered, the ecclesia developed a mode of working through representation – which is never about absolutes, but is always about relationships which can be focussed and fruitful. This complex of fruitful relationship was explored by Dionysius the Areopagite in the notion of a Celestial Hierarchy. Too often in the contemporary world 'hierarchy' is critiqued as being a system of subordination and inequality. The power of 'lordship' which Jesus criticised in the rulers of the Gentiles. In fact the hierarchy of Dionysius was an exploration of the dynamics of divine ordering – the proper meaning of the term. Within such ordering there are different and discernible roles and responsibilities – of different dimensions. Yet all these inter-relationships, including those that seem to express oversight or dependency, in fact contribute to a holistic mutuality. A simple model would be that of the family.

This would be the core for Paul's image of the Body, involving unseemly and dependent parts, as well as more obviously directional ones – all expressing the way and the will of the One Head (1 Corinthians 12). In the same way, the image chosen by Jesus, of a Heavenly Kingdom being revealed on earth, modelled a similar sense of unity in diversity, the direction of the Father uniting and freeing different contributions and responsibilities.

Because the drive and guide for hierarchy, or social ordering, is humility, the richness of complexity and coordination can co-exist – as in the paradox of one crucified yet raised up. Trusting in the Father through the prayer "not my will but Thy will be done". This is the dynamic of social ordering which the ecclesia is called to enable and to represent.

The tools of such a dynamic, entrusted (consecrated) to particular Representatives, consist of signs/ritual, poetry exploding prose, and the blessing of moments – all in the spirit of humility and negation of self. This is the working and energy of a doulocracy: slaves trusting the Master's often inscrutable will. . And yet such bowing down before the mystery presented in the Lordship of Jesus Christ is always accompanied by a spirit of expectancy and the confidence of hope which can thereby crystallise into faith – the faith which dares to be embraced by love. We love because He first loves us (1 John 4:10).

In this way the role of Representation embodies and ministers paradox:

Of not knowing: yet knowing enough

Of not seeing: yet glimpsing Glory

Of sacrificial service: yet being raised up higher

Of embracing the not: yet being made confident in the fruitful reality of the now.

Such is the syllabus of the ecclesia as a workshop of salvation.

This ministering of paradox guards against a totally unwieldly and unfocussed pluralism (the liberal false goal of absolute freedom and toleration). The key is the focus on the source, origin, foundation of truth (John 1:14) which is the touchstone for quality control on behaviour, nourishment, and believing that includes the positive acceptance of paradox. This is faith rooted in the Genesis account of a God who creates all things out of nothing, and in the Johannine account of a God who creates all creatures through His Word. Diversity as one expression of unity.

These elements of 'Representation', in persons, texts and practices consecrated for such purposes (the tools of the workshop of salvation), are witnesses to the mystery of God's Providence – that whatever unfolds, however apparently incoherent, can be received fruitfully. Transformed by a Grace that can overcome even sin, suffering, and death. The key is prayer – the attempt by those in the ecclesia to discern, accept and be shaped by God's working, both negative and positive. Paul explores this amazing truth in Romans 8.

The most challenging and inspiring image of such a reality is presented in the New Testament witness to the crucifixion and revelation of Resurrection to some followers – that they could be apostles to all the world (Matthew 28). They become representatives of this workshop process of slave-like service to the needs of others in order to witness to a deeper connectivity and common purpose which they have tasted and glimpsed. The coming of the kingdom of Heaven on earth.

To access such Revelation, the primary agenda for the health of the ecclesia and its workings is the full and frank recognition of sin. Such missing of the mark for which creatures and creation are intended is not all about the signs of evil and the inscrutable element of the will of God. Much of the sin with which humankind is confronted is the outcome of human freedom and the reality of the Fall. The continuing temptation to put the flesh (self) at the centre as measure and guide.

Nonetheless, the Good News of the Gospel is that despite tending to make such 'choices', individually and collectively, human souls are indwelt by the light of the world (John 1:9-18) and therefore possess the power to recognise wrong, repent and return to the Lord in worship and in self-sacrificing service.

The weakening of this stark and challenging reality of sin needing salvation in a twenty-first century dominated by soft power, toleration, pluralism and faith in humanity per se, is a serious impediment to the proper and fruitful functioning of the workshop that the ecclesia is called to model.

This is why the workshop is called into existence – to recognise and celebrate the central paradox of Grace. The mystery that everything 'good' in human beings is of God – part of the evolution of creation into a fuller salvation. But there remains the paradox that in ascribing all good to the Grace of God, there has to be a recognition of the challenge to human beings to accept responsibility for acknowledging and accepting their freedom to choose, and often to choose selfishly.

"But by the grace of God I am what I am, and his grace toward me has not been in vain. On the contrary, I worked harder than any of them—though it was not I, but the grace of God that is with me."
1 Corinthians 15:10

This paradox takes the Christian journey into the deep territory of the Person – and relationship that is essentially personal: with God and with others.

The mystery of a love that demands obedience while at the same time that same love supplies the means to be obedient. This transaction in Love explains why the image of marriage had been so important for the teaching and the identity of the Christian Church. The very different 'parties' of God and His people, can be joined, despite and yet through differences of being and capability – so that what from a human perspective appears as limitation and incompleteness can be experienced as the possibility and reality of fulfilment. But the coming together of differences needs to be 'worked at' – through committed relationship. This is why an important watchword of the workshop of ecclesia is formation. The form in which the person or group finds itself is able to own incompleteness and become more open to a process of pruning and renewed nourishment that leads to growth and new life – by undertaking the risk of mutual indwelling. (John 15:1-11), i.e. the solidarity of salvation.

It is this working process which means that there will always be a serious difference between the Christian way and the humanistic morality of a 'secular' worldview. Hence the huge gap which modern people tend to feel exists between the Beatitudes and what is seen to be attainable moral behaviour and values. The latter seeks to be 'realistic' in terms of human experience as a measurable entity, which can be seen to be 'practical' in terms of formulating achievable outcomes. A very earthbound agenda, pursued through the working of aims and structures.

By contrast the workshop of ecclesia invites the human heart to own and pursue 'ideals' – headlined in the Beatitudes – potential sensed in the soul but seemingly unattainable because of the confusion which seems to be caused by the essentially paradoxical nature of the clash between hope and pragmatism. The Christian way, often costly, is to accept and pursue the priority of the highest imaginable potential – for others, and through others for the self – all available only through the unmerited and yet always proffered gift of Grace. This grace which is unveiled in the workshop, is 'prevenient' – the goal is God's before it is ours.

Therefore participation in the workshop of ecclesia is a personal responsibility, from which social responsibility emerges. However, paradoxically, the personal tends to be formed by the context of the social (family, neighbourhood, nation, global, faith community).

In this way every 'workshop' of ecclesia is a site of supernatural formation for the person, the society, inter-relation with others: all within the prevenient Grace of God. Such truth is manifested in the earthly ministry of Jesus Christ as Lord – hence the centrality of scripture and of sacraments for the working of the ecclesia: fragmentary resources within Creation as key to the unfolding wholeness of salvation. The connectivity is within the life of the Holy (whole making) Spirit.

Thus Augustine stated that *"every man, from the commencement of his faith, becomes a Christian by the same grace by which that Man from his formation became Christ."*[2]

This is the God who invites His children into a moral order –
for free and responsible persons, who, at every moment, might
be challenged:

- To discern and own failure and limitation – humility and
  repentance (Matthew 4:17).

- To follow the witness of the Son *"I lay down my life..."*
  (John 10:17-18).

- To own prevenient Grace – the highest hope which turns
  faith into love: the call of the Father. "the Son can do nothing
  on his own, but only what he sees the Father doing" (John
  5:19).

- To respond with renewed obedience to the command which
  enables that love to be most fully and clearly expressed (the
  life of the Holy Spirit, 1 John 4:13-21).

- To express such obedience through the slave-like service
  of the needs of others, according to the example and calling
  of Jesus the Christ (Luke 4:16-19 – the Nazareth
  Manifesto).

- To explore through worship the continuing need for change
  and challenge in order to privilege this kingdom agenda (John
  14:11-26).

This process of the workshop enables entry into the life of the
Trinity, which therefore provides the foundation and framework
for the worship that must be at the core of the workshops
functioning if it is to enable the proper operation of the call
to be ecclesia.

In Christ, love recognises the need in the human context
for law as structures and shaping (katechon) but always emerging

from hearts full of hope, rather that enshrined in statutes imposed by a sense of fear upon recalcitrant and reluctant citizens. The ecclesia as workshop enables this agenda and process to be continually recognised, pursued and 're-worked': through worship, followership and witness for the sake of others. The paradox is that every expression of this gifting by Grace will meet deflation and dysfunction by the apparent 'norms' of the human condition, (the sinful tendency to put self first), so that the spiritual endeavour is always a testing journey into promise, paradox and the process of repentance and renewal. Being thrown to the ground or base in order to own the need to look up to others for support and partnership. The call to be lifted up.

This is why worship is the key to the working of ecclesia – as initiator, touchstone, corrective, refiner, illuminator: and then as challenge, ownership of continuing incompletion, and crying out for forgiveness, healing and restored wholeness. The life of the Trinity offers embrace, embodiment and assurance – through a path of challenge (the way of the cross) change and occasions of blessing.

This is the path of what theology calls atonement: a 'covering' or wiping out' in the Hebrew of the Old Testament, and a 'reconciliation' in the term deployed in the Greek of the New Testament. On three other occasions the word used in the New Testament is propitiation. Thus Paul writes: *"being justified freely by His grace through the redemption that is in Christ Jesus, [25] whom God set forth as a propitiation by His blood, through faith…"* Romans 3:24-25.

Sacrificial self-giving lies at the heart of the spiritual relationship from which flows forgiveness and new life – the prevenient Grace expressed through the continuing discipline of repentance and acceptance of blessing that enables hope to become the kind of faith that can be expressed as love.

The sign of the Blood of the Lamb of God who takes away the sin of the world, is therefore the central 'working' of the ecclesia. A 'working' which enables expression of the power that allows the workshop of salvation to function as a site of blessing and encouragement – for and through followers as 'representatives' to those others who seem to be beyond these bounds, though belief, through behaviour or through apparent unconcern.

In this self-sacrificing Christ, this peculiar Kyrios or Lordship, this slave leadership, and though the sign of His Blood, His broken body, is the hope, the path and the practice of reconciliation. The way of Salvation for an otherwise wayward world. A calling always needing further work.

Thus the ecclesia takes seriously the supreme moment of Confirmation of Resurrection *"He showed them His hands and His side."* (John 20:20). The challenging sign of having been 'worked on'. This is the task particularly of a priestly, representative ministry – a focus and formation for the whole ecclesia, and through that discipleship, for the salvation of the world. Christ comes to *"take away the sin of the world"* (John 1:29) and for its salvation (John 12:21-end). He effects this work through slave-like service of the needs of others for a greater sense of wholeness. Such atonement makes this kind of event continually present and effective within the creation God calls into glory. A truth the world cannot live without. A truth the church is called upon to proclaim afresh in each generation. Love is stronger than death, difference or disagreement. 'Work' that continually produces tangible outworkings of hope, and its expression in 'new life', especially for the most unlikely recipients.[3]

Endnotes

[1] The Wisdom of God, p.116.

[2] Augustine. On Predestination. I XV.

[3] For a more detailed exploration of this workshop see The Word on the Street.

Epilogue

In an age which challenges the legitimacy and effectiveness of institutions, particularly against the absolute measure of individual freedom and flourishing, the church can be seen as increasingly irrelevant – locked into an outdated way of thinking and working. Such an analysis presumes a grossly oversimplified understanding of the nature, function and responsibilities of the church as the Body called by Christ to be agent of the inbreaking kingdom or Reign of God.

Like every structuring of relationships and aspirations for human beings, there will always be a need for systems, processes, marks of identity and targets. But – characteristic and constitutive of the Church as the Body of Christ is the call to frame and use these important tools not as ends in themselves, but as more or less helpful markers for the prior and primary call to manifest the process and power of an indwelling Holy Spirit that forever brings the new life, through change, confession and reception of new things (the Resurrection gifts of Grace).[1]

Thus the church is primarily a workshop – testing, refining and ever opening wider, the possibilities God presents for His saving grace to touch and transform human lives – the unfolding journeys of each of His children. Because of the powerful temptation to seek security and stability for ourselves within the narrower confines of our own experience and 'context' – the heart of this workshop is the dynamic between continuing engagement with 'others' (especially those who know their need and dependency), reflection on such encounters and their challenging, changing implications, and the acceptance of fraction as the necessary means of throwing us down from our 'certainties' into a lower place from which we must look up anew to God and to others, especially to strangers and apparent enemies. The spirituality of the slave. Hence the appropriateness of the ecclesia workshop being termed a doulocracy.

This model represents a colossal head-on challenge to contemporary values based upon a democratic ideal to raise up every individual to be a self aware contributing participant, while reserving huge areas of their life to the sphere of the private. The ideal is for each person to be 'master' or 'mistress' of their own life. Much of the world is then seen, experienced and evaluated as providing 'service'.

Similarly the modern emphasis upon secure, scientific, rational judgement reduces options to the discernible and the manageable. Though, paradoxically, such confidence is continually plagued by rival, competing analyses and paradigms!

The ecclesia as workshop is an increasingly counter cultural space of owning utter dependency – upon God (power and purpose) upon others (because so little has been encountered) and upon the unknownness of the self, society or the cosmos. This utter dependency is owned and explored through worship – in the name of the Lord Jesus Christ. His journey of challenge, creativity and call for change to be open to richer possibilities of relationship in religion, politics and society – provides the material and the model. The incompatibility of this spiritual exploration with the narrower securities constructed by 'the world' results in confrontation and fraction, not least in relation to what the 'church' sometimes seems to be establishing. The humility and humiliation of this model of crucifixion of the bearers of such faith (the way of the cross) in fact allows a greater openness to the realities of Resurrection. The process begins and continues within the workshop of the church – and provides an invitation and an example to those at present outside, and seeking other ways.

As the contemporary world rightly fights the evils of modern slavery, there is an important mystery in the Gospel that highlights the chosen path of the doulos or slave as an especially significant way of ordering the workshop of the ecclesia. Like the central importance of poverty, such a profound sign is in danger of simplified misinterpretation. The Gospel endorses neither poverty nor slavery in their worldly manifestations. But both indicate a radical truth about the Gospel call to follow, to be obedient, to depend upon an Other and on others. In this sense the image of ecclesia as doulocracy - a working space for slaves of the kingdom to serve and support the Gospel – could be a strong image to give confidence to a calling that might throw many contemporary assumptions off balance – and thus open up richer and more fruitful possibilities for more of God's precious children. A call to fight false slaveries by recognising the proper place of slavery in the Divine economy. Something that seems to have been close to Paul's own attempt to call and encourage churches in a time of globalising Empire and widespread pluralisms of religion, morality and politics.

This kind of Christian calling needs to be manifested in local churches, personal spirituality and the 'communion' of workshops that seek to forge a Gospel witness and service for our times.[2]

The dynamic between discerning marks of the 'territory' of the Promised Land, and the continual need for revision and enlargement will always be a necessary challenge and discipline for followers called to be disciples witnessing to the way of apostles – slaves who serve as witnesses and guides. This Christian calling needs a workshop in which to be forged, and then re-forged. The process of fraction by which Eucharistic community is formed and sent out for slave like service of the agenda of the kingdom. The Reign of the Father calls through the way of the Son, in the power of the Spirit. Master, slave and salvation in a rich dynamic.

Endnotes

[1] See The Peace that Passes Understanding.

[2] See The Word on the Street.

www.ingramcontent.com/pod-product-compliance
Lightning Source LLC
Chambersburg PA
CBHW051930240626
47153CB00004B/1439